WAYNE STINNETT

RUTHLESS CHARITY

A CHARITY STYLES NOVEL

Caribbean Thriller Series

Volume 2

2016

Published by DOWN ISLAND PRESS, 2016
Travelers Rest, SC
Copyright © 2016 by Wayne Stinnett

Library of Congress cataloging-in-publication Data
Stinnett, Wayne
Ruthless Charity/Wayne Stinnett
p. cm. - (A Charity Styles novel)
ISBN-10: 0-9981285-0-3 (Down Island Press)
ISBN-13: 978-0-9981285-0-4

Cover Photo by D'July
Graphics by Wicked Good Book Covers
Edited by Tammi at Larks & Katydids
Final Proofreading by Donna Rich
Interior Design by Colleen Sheehan, WDR Book Designs

This is a work of fiction. Names, characters, and incidents are either the product of the author's imagination or are used fictitiously. Any resemblance to actual persons, living or dead, businesses, companies, events, or locales is entirely coincidental.

Most of the locations herein are also fictional, or are used fictitiously. However, I took great pains to depict the location and description of the many well-known islands, locales, beaches, reefs, bars, and restaurants in the Keys, to the best of my ability.

DEDICATION

Dedicated to my sister, Vickie Sicilia and her husband Fred. As the oldest of four kids, the rest of us being boys, she had a tough go of it at times. As we grew older, she included me in her circle of friends, though she was in high school and I in junior high. About then, Fred and I became friends. Later as adults, she became the anchor, the one whose home we went to for Thanksgiving dinner. She took care of my youngest brother, through several bouts of cancer and has always been there for all of us. There's a little of Vickie in Charity. Thanks, Sis.

"The moment we believe that success is determined by an ingrained level of ability as opposed to resilience and hard work, we will be brittle in the face of adversity."
- Joshua Waitzkin

If you'd like to receive my twice a month newsletter for specials, book recommendations, and updates on coming books, please sign up on my website:

WWW.WAYNESTINNETT.COM

THE CHARITY STYLES
CARIBBEAN THRILLER SERIES

Merciless Charity
Ruthless Charity
Heartless Charity (Spring, 2017)

THE JESSE MCDERMITT
CARIBBEAN ADVENTURE SERIES

Fallen Out
Fallen Palm
Fallen Hunter
Fallen Pride
Fallen Mangrove
Fallen King
Fallen Honor
Fallen Tide
Fallen Hero (Winter, 2016)
Rising Storm (Summer, 2017)

The Gaspar's Revenge Ship's Store is now open. There you can purchase all kinds of swag related to my books.
WWW.GASPARS-REVENGE.COM

RUTHLESS
CHARITY

MAP

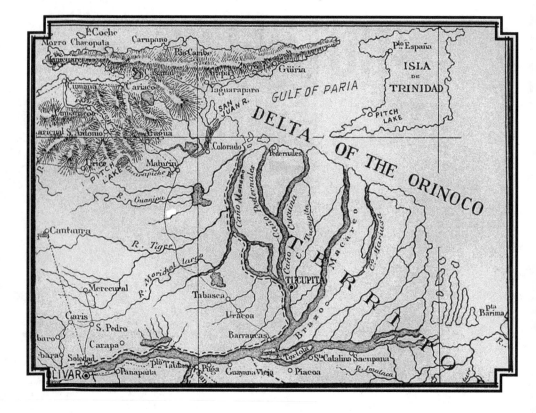

CHAPTER ONE:

Looking up at the night sky, one couldn't help but imagine it being a vast sheet of black velvet with a billion tiny diamonds cast across it. Each star sparkled with its own brilliance and hue. To the south, the long cloudy band of faint stars that made up the Milky Way stretched along the horizon, just a few degrees above it, like a great serpent rising out of the water.

Low on the western horizon, the full moon was just beginning to fall into the sea, seeming larger than usual in the refracted light of the atmosphere. The reflection of the tropical moon stretched to the horizon, shimmering on the calm surface of the sea. Closer, the reflection fragmented and broadened, each ripple in the water nearer the boat creating multiple many-faceted reflections.

A light breeze played across the water from the east-northeast, as it did pretty much year-round in these tropical latitudes. The dry wispy palm fronds rustling against one another in the light air sounded like a mouse scurrying through dry autumn leaves.

Slowly, a classic old wooden sailing sloop motored out of the protected waters of tiny Puerto de Abrigo Marina on the west coast of Isla de Cozumel, Mexico. The boat's lines were simple, yet elegant, its massive wooden mast rising more than forty-four feet above the water, its sails still furled.

In a matter of minutes, the moon would slip into the sea, and soon the sun would take its place. But not before Charity Styles and *Wind Dancer* were many miles from the tourist diving mecca. And not before Charity could enjoy the night sky once more.

With the flip of a switch mounted inside the wheel pedestal, an electric motor whined, driving a hydraulic system which began winching the mainsail from its boom furler, the ticking of the winch drum and gentle luffing of the rising sail making the only sound. The *Dancer* knifed quietly through the still water, her tiny diesel engine adding only a faint burbling sound to the still morning. Once the weight of the boom was lifted, Charity turned around at the helm, and lowered the boom crutch to the aft deck.

Close to shore, the water on the west side of Cozumel was deep—more than deep enough for the *Dancer*, but Charity steered directly away from shore to avoid any chance of colliding with a coral head. Less than a mile out, the bottom dropped precipitously at the edge of the wall, which was the main attraction for thousands of scuba divers. Charity started a slow sweeping turn that would carry the boat further away from shore.

The month before, Charity had spent three days in the little fishing town of Progresso on the northern tip of the Yucatan Peninsula. She'd then come to Cozumel to recuperate from her injuries, swim in the sea, and relax. Yesterday marked four weeks since she'd left the Mexican mainland after the eruption of the San Martin Tuxtla volcano.

She had managed to convince Juan Ignacio to take a few days off from fishing and accompany her to Cozumel. When she'd first arrived back in Progresso, he'd treated and redressed her wounds, not asking any questions. A bullet had grazed the cheek of her ass, and she had a number of scrapes and bruises from a quick descent off the steep mountain peak.

After Juan left, Charity spent the next four days alone on the *Dancer*. She'd come to grips with her actions that night on the mountain, blaming it on her inner demons. Her boss had reprimanded her for being overzealous. He'd sent her to Mexico to track down and kill just one man, the leader of a terrorist cell planning an attack against innocent civilians.

Charity got carried away.

In the end, probably a dozen men met the fate they deserved when the volcano erupted and lava consumed everything in its path—a taste of the perpetual flames she hoped they were now experiencing in Hell.

Late the night before, she'd been instructed to get underway for the island of Trinidad, off the coast of Venezuela. The communication, the first she had received in two weeks, said that more details would come later, but to get underway as soon as possible. She responded in the usual way, giving her approximate date of arrival and saving the email as a draft. Communications from her handler were never sent, just saved in the draft folder of the email server, where only she and her handler had access.

Charity's handler was none other than the Associate Deputy Director for Homeland Security's Caribbean Counterterrorism Command, Colonel Travis Stockwell. He'd devised the simple method of communicating, and rarely resorted to encrypted satellite phones or text messages. It was supposed to prevent any paper or electronic trail, to give his bosses plausible deniability—his bosses being the Secretary of Homeland Security and the President of the United States.

The *Dancer* was equipped with the latest in satellite communication technology, and Charity could access the Internet from just about anywhere in the western hemisphere. Almost immediately, another draft message had been saved, asking if she could speed up the arrival time.

She'd double-checked her calculations at the navigation desk. The distance was about seventeen hundred nautical miles and would have to be made in short hops, island to island, to give her some downtime to rest along the way. The *Dancer* was fast—at least, she was fast for a seventy-two-year-old sailing vessel. Her hull was gel-coated to an ultra-smooth finish, and she slipped through the water with almost no friction. But her top speed in perfect conditions was less than ten knots, meaning sailing time alone would be at least eight to ten days, even with ideal conditions.

Each of the short hops were over two hundred miles. This meant she'd spend at least a full twenty-four hours at the helm, cat-napping through the night, as she'd done to get from Miami to Mexico. Each leg would require a layover to rest. The longest leg would be from Jamaica to Aruba, six hundred miles of non-stop sailing which would take more than three whole days. She'd need plenty of rest before starting that part of the journey and would be worthless on arrival without another day of rest.

She'd replied that her estimate was probably the fastest route to Trinidad, and reminded the director that they'd both agreed this was the most inconspicuous manner to move around the Caribbean Basin. She even challenged him to come to the marina on Grand Cayman in two days and try to find her, knowing that the places she was planning to stop were full of cruisers.

Stockwell had reluctantly approved the arrival time of seventeen to twenty days, telling her that they were still working out the logistics, but she should expect a delivery somewhere along the route she'd outlined.

Charity then spent an hour checking the weather forecasts for her route, something she should have done before giving the director an ETA. The long range forecast for the whole Caribbean, as she'd be crossing it from northwest to southeast, mentioned nothing more than the occasional storms that popped up and disappeared. It was only a month before the start of hurricane season, but when she checked the local forecast between Cozumel and Grand Cayman, she found conditions ideal for a fast passage. She'd decided to start early and be out of the diving areas before the sun came up.

The light breeze filled the sails as they unfurled and Charity killed the engine. Turning southwest, she toggled the winches again, swinging the boom and foresail out to a broad reach, as she angled away from the coast and into deeper water, nearly running before the wind at five knots. Not exactly the *Dancer's* best point of sail.

Sitting in the cockpit, she watched as the last of the moon slipped below the horizon. Its disappearing brilliance allowed the twinkling light from the stars to the west to reach her eye, and soon the whole sky was ablaze with light.

More than an hour later, about two miles off Yucab Reef, Charity turned due south and trimmed the sails once more, to take her past the southern tip of the island. She knew that once she cleared land, the wind would pick up—and when the sun rose and heated the mainland, it would increase even more. She'd be turning east then, and have the wind off her port bow, the *Dancer's* fastest point of sail.

Switching the autopilot on, Charity engaged the computer program that would control sail arrangement and was satisfied that not a single whisper came from the hydraulic winches. The computer confirmed that she'd chosen the most efficient arrangement. A quick look at the radar told her she was alone on the sea for the time being.

As the *Dancer* sailed herself southward, Charity went forward on the port side, checking equipment and rigging all the way to the bow. She double-checked the straps that held her new dinghy in place on the foredeck, thankful that she'd been able to find one while in Progresso.

At the bow, she paused. The sun was only minutes from breaching the horizon, and Charity's shadow was just visible against the foresail behind her. Ahead, the sea looked tranquil. Long rollers no more than a foot high were spaced out ahead, paralleling her direction of travel. The angle of the light from the eastern sky created a shadow below each roller's crest. As they moved beneath the hull she barely noticed, but for the subtle change in the sound of the bow wave slicing through them.

Charity found that she enjoyed letting the computer sail the *Dancer*, and often paused with one foot on the bowsprit. She did so now; gripping the luff of the foresail and leaning forward, she let the wind lift the hair off her shoulders and looked out ahead and all around. Standing there for a moment, she got a rush of freedom unlike anything she'd ever known.

Satisfied that all was well, Charity went down the ladder to the salon to get another bottle of water and slice some fruit to snack on while underway. It would be two long days and two even longer nights, but she'd arrive at Georgetown near sunrise to clear customs in the Caymans.

Back at the helm, Charity left the autopilot on and reclined on the aft port bench, propping a pillow against the wood combing behind her back. Taking a sip from the water bottle, she leaned her head back and looked up again at the stars still visible to the west.

It had been over a month since she'd stolen away before dawn, flying the DHS helicopter to Miami and boarding the *Dancer* for the first time. The experience had been akin to going back to one's childhood home; her uncle had once owned a sailboat almost identical to *Wind Dancer*.

Charity had grown up sailing with her uncle and father nearly every weekend and sometimes all summer long. Uncle Bill had been in the Navy. Her father, Mike Styles, had been a sergeant in the Army. The brothers had served at nearly the same time in Vietnam; both were dead now. Her mother was also dead, for all Charity knew.

Uncle Bill's boat had been laid out slightly different, though it was the same hull design. His had only a single quarter berth under the starboard bench, but it was a double berth laid out cross-hull, with only a couple feet of room at the foot of the bunk, under the cockpit deck, and room enough to sit up at the head, under the cockpit's starboard bench seat. As a child, Charity had loved crawling back into the corner, where only she could fit. There, she could imagine herself to be anything she wanted.

"I wonder," she said aloud, "if I ever imagined myself becoming a government assassin."

There was not another soul on the ocean within miles to hear her words.

CHAPTER  TWO:

One by one, the last of the stars winked out as the sun quickly brightened the sky to the east. Glancing over her shoulder, Charity watched as the dome of the sun began to rise out of the water and suddenly it was nearly full daylight. It took a few more minutes for the bright yellow sun to extract itself from the sea's grasp and begin its daily march across the Caribbean sky.

As the sun climbed higher and the *Dancer* came out of the lee of the island, the wind increased. Charity entered the GPS coordinates for Grand Cayman and, once set, the computer turned the *Dancer* to the new heading, trimming the sails as the boat turned.

The *Dancer* heeled slightly and accelerated, the wind now coming around closer to the bow on the port side. After a moment, Charity checked the knot-meter, smiling to see that they were making an easy nine knots.

The day wore on, uneventful. By mid-morning, the coast of Cozumel had fallen off the radar screen, replaced by a vast empty sea. At noon, Charity went down to the galley to make a sandwich and check the laptop. There was a saved email with an attachment, but no message.

She opened the attachment and saw that it was a short dossier. She skimmed over it quickly, then sent the file to the printer. While it printed, she took the sandwich to her cabin to change into a bathing suit.

Spending an hour each day in the sun was something she'd always tried to do most of her life. For the past month, she'd barely missed a single day. With her hair dyed black, her tan deep and nearly all-over, and her Spanish fluent, she could easily pass for Hispanic. She doubted that even Juan had suspected.

Taking a towel and a pillow, she returned to the cockpit with the printout. She checked the tiny radar display for probably the hundredth time, unsurprised to see an empty screen.

Charity made her way forward and spread the towel on the foredeck next to the mast, propping the pillow against the cabin roof. The wind and hot tropical sun felt good against her skin, as she stretched her legs out and leaned back against the bulkhead. Taking her time, she read through the five-page report twice, enjoying the feel of the boat as the *Dancer* marched steadily onward.

There wasn't much in the report. Her target was an unknown man in Venezuela. There were no pictures or description of him. Nothing much really to go on, other than the fact that the local indigenous people were afraid of him.

There was a list of several men, some with poor quality photos, who were known associates of her target. Surprisingly, they were all white—fair-haired white men, most with European names.

After about an hour, Charity went below and dressed in regular sailing attire: long pants and a long-sleeved shirt, boat shoes and a long-billed cap. It would be very easy to get too much sun at these latitudes.

Pulling her hair back into a loose ponytail, she took the ladder up to the cockpit and checked the radar again. This time she saw another boat, ahead of her. Instinctively, Charity stood on her toes and looked in the direction the radar indicated. Seeing nothing on the horizon, she sat down and studied the image on the screen. It definitely wasn't a ship. The echo was too small. It seemed to be moving in the same direction as the *Dancer*, but at a slightly slower speed.

Over the next couple of hours, Charity kept watch on the radar screen, looking occasionally in the direction it indicated the other boat to be. She knew she wouldn't be able to see it until it was within three miles, but she kept looking just the same.

During that two hours, the *Dancer* closed the distance from eleven miles to seven. Charity estimated the boat was traveling at only five or six knots, and she would likely overtake and pass it just about the time the sun went down.

A man's voice on the radio startled her. "This is MV *Osprey* to the easterly sailing vessel approaching our stern."

His voice had a no-nonsense professional mariner's tone. She wondered how he could tell the *Dancer* was a sailboat. Glancing up at her sails, she realized that although the other boat was too far away for her to see, the Dancer's mast and sails were probably already visible to the other boat, particularly if it was one of those fly bridge motor yachts.

Charity plucked the mic from its holder on the back of the starboard bench. *"Osprey, Wind Dancer.* Switch and answer seventy-two."

Replacing the mic, Charity picked up her hand-held secondary radio and switched it on, before turning the little knob to change frequencies. She waited a moment and the man hailed her again. Keying the mic, she replied, "This is *Wind Dancer.* Go ahead *Osprey."*

"Hello, *Wind Dancer.* Josh Alexander and family here, out of Palm Beach, Florida. We're on our way to Grand Cayman, and the engine's running a little hot."

Charity wondered for a moment what it was the man wanted of her. Cruisers were a social bunch, but if he were to break down, she couldn't very well tow his boat.

"Hi, Josh. I'm Gabriella Fleming out of Miami," Charity said, using her alias and a slight Cuban accent. "Also headed to Grand Cayman. I'm not sure how I can help."

"We thought about turning back, but dropping back to six knots seems to have helped. I figure you're going to pass us in a couple of hours, but we should still be in radio range of one another until you get close enough to hail Grand Cayman. Would you mind relaying a message, should we break down?"

Charity considered the situation. She didn't like the idea of just sailing past a boat in distress, even if she was able to stay in radio contact with them.

"I'm in no hurry, Josh," she finally said into the mic. "Once I catch up with you, I'll stay with you until we're both in radio range of help, probably late tomorrow night."

A woman's voice came over the radio, relief obvious in her every word. "This is Tonia Alexander, Gabriella. We'd be very grateful for the company."

"Not a problem, Tonia. Glad to help any way I can."

The woman stayed on the radio, and they talked occasionally over the next few hours as the *Dancer* slowly reeled in the slower boat.

When the radar indicated that they were only three miles apart, Charity took her handheld VHF and binoculars with her as she went up the port side, checking the rigging and equipment. At the bow, she paused. Ahead, she could just make out the Alexanders' boat on the horizon.

Through the binoculars, it appeared to be a trawler with a fly bridge and aft-cabin. It had a dark blue hull, white topsides, and a dark blue Bimini top that covered both the bridge and the sundeck over the aft cabin. Charity could make out three people on the bridge; a man seemed to be at the helm, and two women in seats flanked him.

As Charity watched, a fourth person emerged from the cabin and went up the ladder to the fly bridge—a third woman, it seemed. The woman went to the aft rail and looked back toward *Wind Dancer* with her own binoculars and waved.

Charity waved back before returning aft, though she wasn't sure the woman could see her. Back at the helm, she checked the GPS and saw that the *Dancer* had traveled nearly a hundred miles since departing Cozumel early that morning. If she maintained this speed, she'd make Grand Cayman several hours before sunrise, day after tomorrow. That meant laying off for a few hours, since the customs and immigration office maintained normal business hours. She could pay the special attendance fee and clear in when she arrived, but few cruisers did that—and not being noticed or remembered was important to her mission. So, slowing down a little wasn't going to hurt her timetable at all.

Less than two hours later, with an hour of daylight left, Charity came abeam on the upwind side of the slower-moving trawler. Switching control of the sail arrangement from automatic to manual, she furled a third of the large foresail, which brought her speed down to match the *Osprey*.

Tonia's voice came over the little hand-held radio. "Are you still on seventy-two?"

"Yes, Tonia. I'm on a hand-held, so I can leave the main radio on sixteen."

"I was about to go below and start dinner. Would you all like to join us?"

Charity had gotten to know the woman a little over the last few hours. She'd learned that the Alexanders were traveling with their two daughters, who had just graduated college and high school. The older daughter was planning a wedding in the fall, and the younger one would be going off to college. The coming summer, Tonia had explained, would likely be the last the four of them could go cruising, something the girls loved.

Though she'd learned quite a bit about the Alexanders, Charity hadn't even told Tonia she was traveling alone.

"I'm a solo sailor, Tonia. so it's just me. Do you think it's wise to shut the engine down?"

"Josh says it'll be fine. He wants to let it cool down a bit, so he can add some coolant before it gets dark and check the strainers."

"In that case, sure," Charity said. "I was just about to make a sandwich and eat at the helm."

"If you're solo, how do you sleep?" Tonia asked.

"Short cat-naps at the helm with the auto-pilot engaged."

There was a short moment of silence before Tonia's voice came over the radio again. "Dinner will be ready in about thirty minutes. Heave to when you're ready, and we'll come alongside to tie off."

A break would be a good idea, Charity thought, remembering her first attempt at a long-distance sail and how tired she'd become.

Switching off the autopilot, she turned slightly toward the other boat as she keyed the mic. "I'll be alongside in a minute and drop the sails."

A moment later, still a hundred feet away from the other boat, Charity toggled the two switches that controlled the furlers, and the sails came down quickly. By the time they were fully furled, she was only fifty feet away and the Osprey had come to a complete stop.

Charity went up the starboard side, dropping fenders over the rail, as Josh maneuvered closer. She could now see that it was a Mainship pilothouse trawler, a very sturdy-looking vessel.

In minutes, the two daughters—both very pretty blondes—had the two boats secured together. Tonia came out of the cabin and met Charity at the rail, extending her hand. "Welcome aboard, Gabriella."

Charity took the offered hand and said, "Please, my friends call me Gabby."

CHAPTER THREE:

The compound was quiet. It usually was, during the hours before sunset. Leon Himmel stood on the front porch of the main house, looking out over the vast expanse of the courtyard. It was his job to make sure things stayed quiet—at least inside the fence. Outside, the jungle had full control.

Situated on the northern end of a huge island in the *Caño Manamo*, the compound was only two kilometers from the northern point of the island, where the two branches of the river came back together. The other end of the long island was fifty kilometers to the southeast. The Manamo itself was the northern distributary of the mighty Orinoco River, into which most of the smaller Venezuelan rivers flowed. The great delta to the east was nearly uninhabited, save for a few backward indigenous tribal settlements.

A man approached the front of the house, riding an ATV. He stopped and shut the machine off before mounting the steps. Taller than Leon, he was also much broader in the shoulders. His shoulder-length dark blond hair, two-day beard, and unkempt clothes contrasted sharply to Leon's own neatly coiffed appearance.

"Some of the farmers along the river are giving us problems," the man said as he stepped up onto the porch. He spoke in German.

"What kind of problems, Karl?"

"Cooperation problems," the bigger man replied, leaning against a post. "The group closer to town, they fear the authorities."

"Babo will not like this."

"That's why I came straight over when I saw you on the porch," Karl replied. "I do not want to be the one to tell him."

Karl turned on his boot heels and started down the steps. As he was about to get back on the ATV, Leon's voice stopped him. "Wait. Was there one farmer out of the group that was more vocal?"

"Yes," Karl replied, sitting down on the seat and producing a pack of cigarettes from his shirt pocket. He shook one out of the pack, lit it with a big silver lighter, and looked up at Leon. "The old man who grows cassava on the land between the rivers—about a hundred morgen of good bottom land where the main river curves sharply, five kilometers before Tucupita."

"Good land," Leon agreed, thinking. "What is this man's name?"

"Vicente Navarro. He is Ye'kuana, and reputed to be a buyei."

"He is the leader of this group?" Leon asked.

"Not in the true sense of the word," Karl said. "But as a shaman of the canoe people, he is revered."

"Who is his biggest rival?"

"Rival? In what way?"

"A nearby farmer," Leon replied. "Someone who also grows cassava."

Sitting back, Karl crossed his arms over his broad chest, his brow furrowed in thought. "The next piece of land south of Navarro's land. A man called Miguel Anders."

"Four men, including yourself," Leon said. "I will meet you at the dock at sunrise and go with you to meet with both of them again."

The corners of Karl's lips turned up slightly. Not really a smile, but more like a sneer. He turned the key, started the ATV, and nodded to his boss. Then he turned the four-wheeler around and drove toward the rutted road that would take him to the back of the five-thousand-acre compound, where his and the other worker's quarters were located.

The compound itself had been built and settled during the mid- 1940s, the whole five-thousand-acre tract purchased outright from the corrupt Venezuelan government. Logging operations had begun immediately, and the northern five hundred acres were mostly cleared in less than a year. The giant caracoli trees, a dense hardwood that grew to over forty meters in height and almost two in diameter, were felled and milled. The lumber was used to build a tall barrier from shore to shore, effectively cutting the land off from the rest of the island. Houses were built, along with a church and school and the small community of Germanic settlers had thrived in obscurity for the next sixty years.

"Was that Aleksander?" a voice behind Leon asked. He started slightly, then turned to face his boss.

"Yes, Babo. There is trouble at one of the farms. I am going with Karl in the morning to resolve it."

The land baron stepped out onto the porch from the open doorway. A handsome man with brown hair and piercing blue eyes, he looked like an ordinary business-man, dressed in a crisp linen shirt and blue tie, with dark blue slacks. The local indigenous people saw him differ-ently. They saw him as the precursor of pain and suffer-ing, much the same as they'd seen his father before him.

"What sort of trouble, Leon?"

"Just a couple of malcontents. I can handle it."

The man's eyes flashed only for a moment, but in that moment Leon was frightened. "I asked what sort of problem."

Leon swallowed hard. He'd worked for this man for nearly four years, and for his father for four years before that, until the old man died. The two had known one another all their lives, and grown up together on the com-pound. They were three years apart in age, but in this small community of only eight square miles, walled off from the rest of the world, there were few secrets.

"One of the farmers," Leon replied. "The old man, Navarro. He is resisting."

"What is it you plan to do?"

Leon shrugged. "What we have always done. Make an example of one to ingratiate the other."

"When it is done," Babo said, turning to go back inside before the mosquitoes swarmed, "bring the old man here so I might talk to him further."

Early the next morning, Leon was waiting at the dock when Karl arrived. Leon knew the three men in the boat with Karl. He knew everyone in the community; small though it was, there was a hierarchy and these men were the workers.

The boat was nearly new, one of the benefits of a new business venture the community was now involved in. A custom-built aluminum ten-meter tunnel hull with a powerful jet drive outboard engine, it could easily glide across the constantly shifting sandbars of the Manamo. In fact, it could fly across water so shallow that, if it ran aground, the men would only have to get out; the reduced weight would allow them to push it to the four-inch depth it needed with a thousand pounds aboard.

Their fathers and grandfathers, who had founded the community, started in the timber business; many of them had been former lumbermen and builders before the war. By the end of the 1940s, they'd moved on to mining in the nearby mountains. For decades, the men and women of the community got rich off the natural resources and the people.

Two years before, Babo had said that the forestry and mining operations were too visible and required the people of the community to mix too much with outsiders. Upon seeing that there was a world outside the dangerous waters of the river that surrounded them on three sides and the wall to the south, many men—and some women—had left the community.

Karl turned the boat and came up alongside the newly constructed dock, where Leon waited. Without a word,

Leon stepped down into the boat and went forward to stand beside Karl at the helm.

Karl pushed the throttle forward and the long, wide boat leapt out of the water, all five men holding on. In seconds, the boat was skimming the flat brown surface at high speed, weaving through the curves, headed upriver. With the boat's ultra-shallow draft, the only sandbars Karl had to worry about were those on which the crocodiles had hauled out to wait for the morning sun.

The trip up-river only took twenty minutes, and soon the boat slowed, settling into the deeper water in the middle of the river.

"This is Navarro's land," Karl said, sweeping his arm toward the west.

With the boat barely moving against the great current, Leon looked out over the fields. The whole island was a flood plain, the soil rich in nutrients brought down from the mountains. It had been over twenty years since the last really big flood, though smaller annual floods were a way of life, and the cassava plants flourished.

"And this other man? Anders? Where does his land start?"

Karl nudged the throttle and the boat moved a little faster against the current. They reached a point of land where the river bent toward the west. Just off the point, Karl slowed the boat until they were again motionless, matching the current.

"This point is the boundary between the two farms," Karl said, motioning toward the fence line. "Anders's spread is a triangle. The fence between the two goes southwest from this point.

"How far inland are the two men's homes?" Leon asked.

Karl shook a cigarette from his pack and lit it, blowing the smoke upward before answering. "Just a few hundred meters. They are very close to one another."

"Family? Workers?"

"Navarro lives alone. Two young men from town come out every morning to help him in the fields. Anders has a family—a wife, three sons, and a daughter. The oldest son and a boy from town help him."

"We will go ashore here," Leon said, "on Navarro's side of the point."

Turning and angling the boat toward a deep spot near shore, Karl advanced the throttle a little. A small dugout canoe was pulled partway up onto the low bank in the small cove, sheltered from the current.

"Run it over," Leon instructed.

Karl did as he was told—not that he had to be told. He had intended to crush the canoe anyway. Just before making contact with the side of the dugout, Karl hit the throttle, and the bow rose up over the side of the much smaller boat.

The crack of the dried wood as the side caved in sounded like a small-caliber rifle shot. Karl pulled the throttle back to neutral, just as the big aluminum boat's bow rode up onto shore. He killed the engine as two of his men climbed up onto the bow and jumped down to the riverbank. Within minutes, the men had the boat tied off to two small trees, though it was unnecessary. The boat was resting on top of the dugout, which sat submerged on the mucky bottom.

"Take two men," Leon said. "Go to Anders's house and bring anyone you find there to the fence between the two houses." He pointed to the largest of Karl's three men, a man he only knew as Rolph, and said, "You come with me."

They split up, Karl and his men crossing the fence and heading inland on one side while Leon and Rolph made their way toward a low hut on stilts.

Walking toward the thatched shanty, between the rows of newly planted cassava, Leon looked all around but saw nobody. When he and Rolph reached the hut, they still had not seen anyone. The structure itself sat on pilings, with the floor about two meters above the ground. Its walls were a hodgepodge of materials, some corrugated tin, some bare planks, but mostly saplings no thicker than a man's wrist, cut to length. The low roof was made of palm fronds, less than two meters above the floor on the four sides and perhaps four meters at the center.

"Navarro!" Leon called out to the stilt hut.

Hearing shouts from the south, not far away, Leon turned toward the sound and saw Karl and the other two men approaching. They herded a small, half-naked woman carrying an infant, with two other children walking in front of her.

By the time Leon reached the fence, the shouts had brought the others out of the fields. A man and two boys came running up from behind Karl, and an old man with two younger men came from Navarro's field. Soon, the field workers were gathered with the others at the fence.

"Which one is Navarro?" Leon asked Karl.

Pointing, Karl replied, "The old man. And that is Anders."

The older man stood slightly away from the group and seemed to be patiently waiting. Leon moved toward him, expecting him to cower, but he did not. His hair was long, past his shoulders, and completely white. He did not wear his bangs cut short like most of the indigenous people in the area. His skin was dark and the lines in his face were many. He stared at Leon, his dark eyes unyielding and inscrutable.

"You are Vicente Navarro?" Leon asked in broken Spanish.

"Yes," the old man replied, "and I speak English."

"Well, la-di-fucking-da," Leon nearly shouted in English. "Karl tells me you and some others do not want to raise the crops we want to buy."

Navarro simply stared back. At five-nine and a trim one hundred and sixty-five pounds, Leon towered over the diminutive old man.

"Why not?" Leon asked him.

"I am not a coca farmer," Vicente replied, shrugging his shoulders. "I grow cassava for my people."

"Your people?" Leon said, stepping closer and looking down at the old man. "You are Ye'kuana. These others are not your people."

"Ye'kuana, Warao, Pemon, Yanomami—we are all the children of Wanadi and the forest."

"You are going to grow what I tell you, old man."

Vicente merely stared back in silence.

Anders spoke up, in Spanish. "We wish only to grow our food and be left in peace."

Leon turned to face him across the fence. "Peace?" he asked, slowly drawing his large revolver from a holster at his waist. "There will be no *peace*, if you do not grow the coca."

Striding toward the fence, Leon raised the gun.

Anders cowered, his head drooping.

Leon pointed the gun at the woman; she gathered the two children behind her, expecting the worst.

Moving the weapon quickly, Leon fired a single shot, hitting Anders's field hand squarely in the chest. The large-caliber bullet lifted the boy off his feet, sending him sprawling backward in the dirt, dead before he hit the ground. The woman screamed and ran toward the dead boy.

Leon slowly turned toward Navarro. "If I come back, I will kill you all and give your land to a farmer who has more sense." Holstering his revolver, he started back down the path toward the boat, and called over his shoulder: "Throw the body in the river!"

Karl pointed to one of his men, who bent and grabbed the dead boy by one wrist and began to drag the body toward the river. The rest of the men went ahead, none wanting to miss what would happen next.

At the river bank, with the woman and children weeping loudly, another of Karl's men took the dead boy's feet and the two men tossed the body out into the water. There, it floated for a moment in the still water near shore.

After just a few seconds there was movement, as if the boy's muscles twitched. A few seconds later the body began a series of steady spasms, and within a minute the water around it began to roil and turn red with blood, as piranha swarmed in from all over this part of the river, drawn by the splash and the scent of blood in the water. Black piranha, called *caribes* by the indigenous people, could grow to nearly a foot long. And they had voracious appetites.

CHAPTER FOUR:

After a tour of the Alexanders' boat and a nice dinner served on the aft sundeck, Angela and Vanessa asked Charity if they could see *Wind Dancer*. Charity thought quickly, and decided there was nothing out in the open that might alarm the girls or their parents.

"Sure," Charity replied and turned to Josh and Tonia. "Care for some after-dinner wine?"

They readily agreed, and the five of them stepped over into the *Dancer's* cockpit. Charity led the way down the ladder to the salon as the two girls marveled at the *Dancer's* interior appointments. They were particularly impressed with the electronics.

"We have the usual navigation equipment," Angela said. "Even auto-pilot. But what happens when you're resting at the helm and the wind changes?"

Turning her laptop on the desk of the little nav-station, Charity explained. "I don't know how it works, only that it does. There's a program on my laptop that's connected to all the navigation and electronics systems, including the auto-furlers. The wind could change all it wants, and the computer will read the direction and speed and correct the sail arrangement."

Charity suggested sitting in the cockpit and pointed out to Josh where the wine glasses were. Opening the small cooler on the port side, she searched through several bottles until she found what she wanted.

Back on deck, Charity opened the wine and handed the bottle to Josh, noticing that he'd brought five glasses. He poured a smaller amount into the glass of his youngest daughter, who rolled her eyes in a manner typical of girls her age.

Relaxing in the cockpit as the sun went down, Charity listened to the banter among the family members, contributing on occasion. The older girl reminded Charity of herself when she was that age—which seemed like a lifetime ago.

"I have an idea," Angela said to Charity. "Since you're going to slow down and keep pace with our boat, maybe I could ride with you? Vanessa and I both take turns at watch on our boat. You'd be able to get more rest."

Tonia smiled, letting Charity know she trusted her.

If she only knew what I do for a living, Charity thought.

It was definitely not a good idea, and Charity knew it. She tried to quickly think of a polite way to decline, with dozens of scenarios running through her mind. The director still hadn't let her know when to expect the drop-off to replenish her armament and a few other things. He'd probably make it a night drop, but he'd never struck her as impulsive. He seemed to plan things out further than a few hours, so she doubted it would be tonight.

Nothing she could think of to avoid having a stranger, a civilian non-combatant, on board would make sense. She liked the young woman, so reluctantly agreed.

"Sailing is different than power-boating," Charity said. "Do you have sailing experience?"

"Not a lot," Angela replied. "I dated a guy in high school who sailed, and I learned a lot from going out on his boat."

"Okay," Charity agreed and turned to Josh. "If it's okay with your father."

Josh nodded. "We'll be just a few hundred feet apart, and all she'll really have to do is monitor what's going on, right?"

"Right," Charity replied. "Once the course and speed are set in the computer, it will keep the sails trimmed to maintain it."

"It's settled then," Tonia said. "We should get underway."

In minutes, the girls cast off the lines, as Josh and Charity started the engines on the two boats. Once they were turned back onto the right heading, they angled apart to a safe distance and Charity used the manual switch to unfurl the *Dancer's* sails, keeping the foresail reefed, so as not to out-distance the Alexanders' boat.

Josh hailed her on the hand-held. "Are you still on this channel, Gabby?"

Charity picked up the radio and replied, "Yes, we are. How is your water temperature?"

"Running normal. I'm going to push it up to our usual cruising speed of eight knots and see if it holds."

Slowly, the *Osprey* began to pull away. After a few minutes, Josh came back on the radio. "She's running just a little hotter than usual, but well within the normal range."

Reaching down, Charity toggled the switch to fully unfurl the foresail. *Wind Dancer* came alive in the steady wind and began to slowly overtake the Alexanders' boat. When the *Dancer* had closed the distance to a hundred yards, Charity stood up.

"Take the helm a minute," she said to Angela. When the girl was at the wheel, Charity slipped down to the salon and opened the laptop computer. She set the program to maintain eight knots, and heard the whirring sound of the foresail furler as it reefed slightly to maintain the slower speed. She took a spare safety harness from the storage cabinet below the nav-desk and returned to the cockpit.

"Put this on," she said, handing Angela the safety harness. "Every hour while you're on watch, I want you to check the rigging and deck equipment to make sure everything on deck is secured. The windward shroud should feel solid when you put your hand on it and the leeward shroud should have just a tiny bit of vibration while underway. Come with me, I'll show you."

Charity clipped and unclipped her safety line along the top cable rail as she moved forward. She checked the rigging and made sure everything on deck was still secured. Angela followed, also using her safety line, paying close attention to everything Charity showed her.

"Notice the difference?" Charity asked when they reached the starboard shroud.

The younger woman put a hand on the rigging and nodded. "The other side felt like it was a solid part of the boat. This side's vibrating like a guitar string."

"Good analogy," Charity said. "A sailboat is a lot like a musical instrument, when the rigging is properly tuned." As they made their way back to the cockpit, she continued, "Unlike a power boat, which forces its way through the water regardless of current or wind, a sailboat moves in harmony with the elements. Like a violin in the hands of an experienced musician, if one part is out of tune, it will tell you."

With the sun slipping below the horizon behind them, Charity and Angela agreed on a watch schedule. Charity would take first watch until midnight, then Angela would take over until four o'clock. Four straight hours of sleep a night for two nights would be easy and Charity knew she'd probably be more rested than if she napped at the helm.

Besides, she thought, *I can sleep twelve hours once we arrive in the Caymans.*

Taking the younger woman below, Charity quickly converted the settee to a bunk and laid out the spare blankets and pillows. "We'll hot bunk in the salon," Charity said. "In case of an emergency, it will be three less steps to get to the cockpit."

Back on deck, Charity settled in at the helm, taking her encrypted satellite phone out of her pocket. She quickly wrote a message to the director explaining what was going on and that she didn't anticipate a delay because of it. Seconds after sending it, she received a reply.

I'll meet you at Harbour House Marina for lunch in two days.
TS

She contemplated asking why, knowing that even Travis Stockwell wouldn't risk bringing a sniper rifle and ammo into the Caymans. She decided not to ask. Whatever it was, it would just have to wait.

She replied with a single word: *Affirmative.*

CHAPTER  FIVE:

When Thurman Napier woke up, he didn't know where he was. Rolling over on the thin mattress, with springs poking into his ribs, he saw the bars and realized he was in jail again. He sat up slowly, the throbbing in his head taking on jackhammer proportions as he massaged his temples and tried to remember how it was he'd been arrested this time.

A clanking noise got his attention, and he looked up. The view through the bars wasn't anything to write home about; all he could see was a blank wall on the other side of the narrow walkway in front of his cell.

The jailer stopped in front of the cell and looked in. "I see yuh awake now. Too bad. I was goin ta rattle di bars. You got a visituh."

As the jailer stepped toward the door and inserted a key, another man moved in front of the cell: a tall man with a graying crew cut. Through the fog in Thurman's brain, he tried to train his one eye on the figure standing in front of him.

The jailer opened the cell door and the man stepped inside.

"Leave us for a minute?" the man asked.

"What the hell are you doing here?" Thurman asked, interrupting the guard as he was about to say something.

"Yuh sure bout dat?" the jailer asked the tall man.

Travis Stockwell turned toward the jailer. "Yes, I'm sure. Go arrange for his release. Whatever bail, fines, or damages he caused, I'll pay for."

The guard left, locking the cell door behind him and muttering under his breath.

"Good morning, Napper," Stockwell said.

"Nobody calls me that anymore, Colonel," Napier replied. "And what the fuck are you doing in Port of Spain?"

Travis moved to the wall and leaned against it, where he could see the door down the narrow hall. He quickly scanned the hallway and then the cell, paying particular attention to the ceilings.

"This is the remand prison," Napier said. "I recognize the cell. Nothing but drunks and pickpockets here. No high-tech security."

Stockwell looked down at the man on the bunk. At fifty-five, Thurman Napier looked like a horse that'd been ridden hard for a very long time and put up wet. His face was a maze of wrinkles and a few scars. The eye patch did nothing to soften his overall demeanor. Scraggly black hair turning gray and a two-week beard, also mostly gray, gave him the appearance of a much older man.

"I came here to hire you," Travis said. "But it looks like I have to get you out of jail first. Again."

"What is it with you, anyway?" Thurman asked. "I don't need or want your help."

"Yeah, I know. You can do or be just about anything you want, Napper. God knows you have the money. Why do you continue to wallow in this cesspool of a life you created?"

"It's my life," Napier responded, rising to his feet. Stockwell was a tall man, nearly six feet. But as Napier slowly reached his full height, stretching and rolling his shoulders like a prizefighter, he was a head taller than Stockwell.

"Look," Travis said, pushing away from the wall and standing by the door. "I need your help, Napper."

"Stop calling me that!" Thurman bellowed. "I ain't been that man for decades."

"No, you're a drunk wharf rat now—sleeping in gutters and dumpsters, picking up the disease of the month from every Trini hooker on the waterfront."

"Insults ain't gonna endear you, Colonel. Just lay out what it is you came here for, so I can tell you to go fuck yourself and this conversation will be over."

"I need a man and a boat. Someone I trust, who can take a shooter upriver to locate, identify, and kill the leader of the brotherhood."

This immediately got Napier's attention. "One man?"

"Not exactly," Travis replied. "Are you interested?"

"Why now? Why, after all the shit they've stirred up down there since before either of us was born, does the government want to get involved now?"

"I never said anything about the government."

"You didn't have to," Napier said, stepping over to the bars and looking down the hall. "You're you."

"Are you interested?" Travis asked again.

Thurman lifted his patch, digging a dirty finger into the empty eye socket and flicking the crust that had collected there to the floor of the cell.

"It was the brotherhood that did this," Thurman finally replied, adjusting the patch. "Yeah, I'll listen to what you have to say. But that's it. I'll listen."

"That's all I ask," Travis said, then turned and yelled down the hall. "Guard! We're ready!"

Twenty minutes later, as the two men walked outside to a waiting car, Thurman said, "I coulda paid my own bail."

"*Wipe This* still running?"

"Fastest boat on the river," Thurman replied. "Even at twenty years old."

"Probably more to do with your knowledge of the river than the boat."

"I already said I'd listen, Colonel. Sucking up is beneath you, anyway."

They got in the car, which Napier immediately recognized as an embassy vehicle. "Head toward the waterfront," Travis told the driver. "Anywhere there's a public pier."

As the car pulled out onto the street, Travis turned to Thurman. "So, what'd the TP King get busted for this time?"

Though his head still hurt, Napier quickly caught on: Stockwell's directive to the driver, and then his asking such an innocuous question. Colonel Stockwell had always been a man of few words; he didn't engage in idle chit-chat.

So Stockwell didn't trust the driver.

"Same old shit, I guess," Thurman replied. "Don't really remember a whole lot. Probably busted up a bar or beat up a city alderman's son."

They rode in silence for a while. "Don't you think you're getting a little too old for that?" Travis finally asked, as the car turned off the road into the parking lot of a fishing pier.

"Ask the twenty-something city alderman's son if I'm too old."

The two men got out and Stockwell told the driver to wait for them. "My friend has to see a man about a boat."

Walking toward the pier, Napier said, "You don't trust the driver? What's this shit about?"

"I don't *know* the driver and I don't trust anyone I don't know. The babo is gaining strength and following. We still don't even know who the hell the man is."

"The son of the old babo," Napier said, matter-of-factly. "Everybody knows that. And the babo is the babo. Doesn't matter who he was before that."

"I'm with a specialized branch of the federal government now," Travis explained. "We—and by that I mean myself and one operative—work in the shadows and get the job done."

Napier stopped in his tracks midway on the pier. It was late morning, and most of the early fishermen had already packed it in. There were only two men still fishing at the end of the pier.

"You're doing wet work now, Colonel?"

"I'm the handler, and I've been told to eliminate the babo."

"Babo's a ghost, man. Some say he doesn't even exist in this world, but can come and go, in and out of it, at will. I know he's flesh and blood, though. At least his father was."

"If he's flesh and blood, he can be killed," Stockwell said.

"Have you ever been up the Manamo, Colonel? The river itself can kill you in half a heartbeat, and the jungle around it is practically impenetrable and just as deadly. There's still people back in those jungles that've never seen a white man or a gun. The brotherhood carved out a huge swath of it, surrounded by the river and a huge, guarded wall."

"My operative isn't without talent and skill."

"And you want me to take him up there?" Thurman asked. "That what you came down here for? Those fuckers'll shoot my ass on sight."

"Then you'll have to not be seen," Travis said.

"Good luck with that, man," Thurman snorted. "It ain't about not being seen up there. It's about not being seen, heard, smelled, or sensed. There's piranha and crocs in the water, and jaguars in the jungle. They know you're there, no matter what you do. And they tell Babo."

"You getting superstitious in your old age?"

"Fuck off, Colonel. You don't know the jungle here."

"I can get you a boat," Travis said. "Faster and tougher than *Wipe This*."

"No such animal. On the Manamo, speed'll kill you dead anyway. A boat's gotta be nimble and able to run shallow enough to glide across a water puddle. The river's plenty wide, but the sand bars are constantly shifting. People've tried hovercraft, but if one errant tree branch snags the skirt and rips it off, you got yourself a fifty-mile-per-hour hunk of shit heading straight for the spot where it's gonna kill you."

"Twenty-eight-foot tunnel boat, with twin waterjet engines."

"That's been done, too," Thurman said, pulling a flask from his pocket and taking a drink. His lips pulled back in a grimace as the fiery liquid burned its way down to his empty stomach. "Sand gets sucked up into the strainers and clogs the cooling system."

"Air-cooled engines," Stockwell said. "A pair of turbo-charged vee-twin motorcycle engines on steroids. A friend came up with the idea, and I had the boat built just for this op. It's yours if you help."

"Motorcycle engines? You gotta be shittin' me. *Wipe This* has twin one-tens."

"Each one produces over a hundred and eighty horsepower."

"Out of a motorcycle engine?"

"Not your standard Harley," Stockwell replied. "They've been specially adapted to work in the boat, with big cooling fans."

"And all I gotta do is take your guy into the jungle and drop him off?"

"You'll do it?" Stockwell asked, leaning on the pier railing and looking out over the water. "I can have the boat here in two days, so you can get used to it. My operator will be here in three."

"Why not bring him in with the boat?"

"*She* is under sail, Napper. Arriving in the Caymans tomorrow. That's another thing. Do you still have that little airfield and hangar?"

"She?" Napier asked, incredulously. "You're sending a woman into that jungle after Babo? Are you fucking nuts?"

"She's not your average woman," Stockwell said. "Now, do you still have the hangar?"

"Sure, but it's nowhere near water for a sailboat to get to."

"In two days, she'll be in the air, arriving here in three."

The big man scratched at his scraggly beard. "No offense, Colonel, but something just don't add up here. In the big picture, the babo's small potatoes. Sure, he's probably raped and killed a bunch of indigenous people down there, and I know for a fact he's killed some of his own and probably done a lot worse than that. But why would the American government put a contract on him?"

"This particular operative," Stockwell began, choosing his words carefully, "has been on sort of a probationary status for a while. This is what you might call a test."

"A test? And you wanna rope me into it?"

"Oh, she's perfectly capable," Stockwell replied. "It's just that on her last mission she sort of went off the reservation."

"Off the reservation? Is that your way of saying overkill?"

Stockwell nodded. "In the literal sense of the word."

"And the Puzzle Palace up in DC wants to do a reboot, but on a smaller scale?"

"Something like that," Stockwell replied. "Are you in?"

CHAPTER SIX:

After the murder by the river, Leon and his men climbed back into the aluminum-skinned boat. The piranha did not take long to consume the body of the small boy, leaving little but tattered clothing over bones.

"Navarro!" Leon shouted as the boat backed off the crushed canoe. "Babo wants to see you at his house tonight when the sun goes down. Do not make him wait."

Vicente looked down at his ruined canoe, shrugged, and walked away toward his hut. Miguel Anders and the others followed him at a distance, the woman still very distraught.

"What will you do, Buyei?" Anders asked the shaman in Spanish, as the two men walked ahead of the others.

Vicente shrugged. "I will go see the babo."

Miguel stopped on the trail for a moment, until Vicente also stopped and turned toward him. "The babo is evil," Miguel said. "He will kill you just for fun. Besides, how will you get there?"

"He killed your harvester to make a point," Vicente said. "He will not kill me, and that was not my only *bongo*."

The two men continued walking toward Vicente's hut. When they reached it, Vicente stirred the cook fire and added more wood. Miguel sent his wife home with the smaller children. The two men, Miguel's oldest son, and Vicente's two young field workers sat down at the fire.

From a bag next to the fire, Vicente produced a long slender pipe and a small pouch. He filled the pipe with dried yopo seeds and lit it with a twig from the fire.

Passing the pipe to Miguel, Vicente said, "A spirit came to me last night, right here on this very spot. She looked like a child of the Wanadi, but inside she radiated a white light."

Miguel pulled slowly on the pipe, relighting it with another twig. Sharing the yopo seed with the buyei was a great honor. Holding his breath for a moment, he gently waved the smoke, curling from the end of the pipe, up and over his head, as he'd seen the old shaman do at times. The field workers were not yet men and not permitted to partake of the yopo.

"Did this spirit tell you something?" Miguel asked, unsteadily passing the pipe back to Vicente. He was already feeling the effect of the hallucinogenic seeds. Miguel had lived on the land next to Vicente for many years, but they rarely spoke. The older man was a buyei of the boat people and Miguel was a simple peasant farmer of the forest people. Sitting by the fire, smoking the yopo with the old shaman, gave Miguel a feeling of importance.

"Yes," Vicente softly replied. He relit the pipe once more, before continuing in an almost reverent voice "Her appearance was at first confusing to me. Yet I know this spirit was sent by the Mother of the Forest. The spirit said for me to do as the *itoto* tell me. She conveyed that when the time was right, she would descend on our enemy and banish them to the Snake of Being, where they belong."

Miguel nodded his head, pleased that the old shaman already knew what would happen. "It is good, then."

Vicente turned to the older of his two apprentices. "Go to the people. Tell the elders I wish them to meet me here tonight, when *Choco* is directly overhead."

Without a word, the young man rose and ran off toward the river where he'd left his canoe.

"Return to your field, Miguel," the old man said. "I will await another visit from this spirit. Take this *nibora* with you, so that he may continue to work in place of your lost *nibora*."

Together, Miguel and the two boys rose and went in the direction of the low fence separating the land used by the two men. They would work until the sun touched the surrounding treetops, giving the boy from town enough daylight to make it home safely.

Vicente tapped the ashes from the pipe and repacked it. Before lighting it, he took a charred twig that had fallen away from the fire and used it to make jagged lines low across his forehead and cheeks. From his pack, he removed a cloth that was dyed red using achiote seeds. Vicente carefully folded the cloth from corner to corner and rolled it into a bandana, which he then tied around his head. Satisfied, he relit the pipe and drew deeply, swathing the smoke over his face and head.

Eyes closed, he waited for the light spirit to return

CHAPTER SEVEN:

Wind Dancer and Osprey arrived in Cayman waters several hours before daybreak. Charity and Josh both called ahead to Port Authority and were told there was an overtime charge to gain entry after hours.

"Can we anchor in North Sound until the Customs office opens?" Josh asked.

The Port Authority man directed both boats to an anchorage in North Sound, near Governor's Creek. He explained that they could clear in at Georgetown, if the cruise ships weren't in the way, or at Cayman Yacht Club.

Anchoring in twelve feet of water, off Governor's Creek, both boats flew the quarantine flag, signifying that they had not yet cleared customs. The engine in the Alexanders' boat had continued to run slightly hotter than usual the whole way, but within its normal operating range, so it hadn't been a big concern.

With little else to do, Charity put her new dinghy in the water, with help from Angela. Leaving the boat wasn't legal and Charity knew it, but she needed to get separated from the Alexander family. She and Angela motored quietly over to where the *Osprey* was anchored less than a hundred feet away. Tonia already had breakfast ready for the whole group.

"I want to thank you for all your help, Gabby," Josh said, as Charity stepped over into the *Osprey's* cockpit.

"A pleasure," Charity replied, still using her slight Cuban accent. "Having Angela aboard made my passage a lot more restful. She's a fine sailor."

Tonia insisted that she join them for a quick breakfast, but as soon as they finished eating, Charity said her goodbyes and returned to the *Dancer*, telling the Alexanders that she wanted to get some rest before checking in with Immigration and Customs.

"I'm going into the creek as soon as it's light," Charity told Josh. "I'm meeting a friend at the yacht club for lunch."

"Too steep for us," Josh said. "We'll clear in at the Georgetown dock and grab one of the free Port Authority mooring balls."

Charity liked the Alexanders, but needed to be clear of them before meeting with Director Stockwell. She really was tired, but she also needed to check for a message from him. The director had said he'd meet her somewhere on Grand Cayman this morning. Opening her laptop, she signed in on the secure email client and there was indeed a saved message in the drafts folder.

> *Lunch at noon. Casa Havana, at the Westin on
> Seven Mile Beach.*
> *—TS*

After deleting the message, she typed in a one word reply— *Affirmative*—and saved it in the folder.

Lunch? *How is he going to bring a rifle and the other gear to a restaurant?* Charity wondered.

This was outside the parameters of what they'd discussed beginning several months ago. They'd agreed from the outset that there would be no further contact with any of the team members after she left. Contact with the director himself would be kept at a minimum, and only through the saved email drafts and an occasional text message or phone call on her secure satellite phone.

For the next hour, Charity cleaned and straightened up the cabin, converting the settee back to a table. Finished, she stripped down to just a tee-shirt and climbed into her bunk for a few hours of sleep, still wondering why the director wanted a face-to-face meeting.

<hr />

Light was shining through the starboard porthole when Charity awoke. The narrow shaft of light fell on the dark-stained wooden hatch of the hanging closet, the angle telling her it wasn't very long past sunrise. Checking her watch, she confirmed that it was just past eight o'clock local time.

Charity rose, turned on the hand-held VHF, and contacted Port Authority to ask about entry at the yacht club. The man told her he'd relay the message to Immigration, Customs, and Mosquito Control. They'd be happy to come to her at the marina, and would probably be there in thirty minutes or less.

She contacted the marina to see about renting a slip until the following morning. The marina operator told her there was plenty of room, and assigned her to a slip with shore power and water hook-ups, very close to the marina office.

"I plan to sleep the day away," Charity said. "I'll be leaving in the morning. Is there a slip further away, where it might be more peaceful?"

The marina operator gave her a different slip number, and directions to it. Dressing quickly in a loose-fitting green halter dress she'd bought in Cozumel, Charity went to the galley to start the coffeemaker, then up to the cockpit with the last of her bananas and a mug of coffee. She noticed that the Alexanders' trawler was already gone.

Minutes later, she had the engine started and pulled the anchor from the sandy bottom, marveling at how clear the water in the sound was. She found her assigned slip easily enough, at the end of the longest pier, and was pleased to see a marina employee waiting to help with the lines as she approached.

Once the *Dancer* was tied up and she'd tipped the young man, she went below to refill her coffee mug, returning to the cockpit to wait for the officials to arrive and grant her entry.

The wait wasn't long; she'd barely finished half of her second cup before the officials arrived. She filled out the required forms, declaring nothing, and the Mosquito Control man went into the salon to spray his chemical fog.

"You must leave the cabin closed up for at least five minutes," the guy in the white jumpsuit told her. "Not to worry, di fog won't hurt you, only di mosquitos."

Charity had reservations about that, and planned to leave the cabin closed and locked while she went to the marina store. Then she'd leave it open for an hour to air out.

The Customs man stamped Charity's passport and she paid the entry fee, then grabbed her oversized shoulder bag and went to the marina office to take care of business, get directions to the Westin, and hopefully buy provisions for the next leg of her journey.

Returning to the *Dancer*, she placed her bag of groceries on the port bench and opened the main hatch. Taking a deep breath, she hurried down the ladder, opening the portholes in the salon and the overhead hatch in the forward stateroom.

Her lungs were burning for oxygen when she grabbed a bottle of water from the refrigerator and climbed quickly back up the ladder. On deck, she exhaled and drew in a few deep breaths. She didn't want to take any chances with whatever chemicals the bug man sprayed.

The morning was still cool. The prevailing southeasterly wind was light, fresh and clean as it blew across the *Dancer's* bow. It carried a mixture of scents from all around the anchorage. She retrieved her hammock from the storage box under the port bench and strung it up under the boom to relax for a while before putting the groceries away.

Feeling not the least bit refreshed after an hour nap, Charity stowed the groceries and walked back down the long dock to the marina office. The man there had assured her that a cab could arrive within just a few minutes to take her anywhere on the island, if one wasn't already parked there.

As she approached the front of the building, a cab was just pulling into the driveway. It stopped in front of the marina office, and a tall, blond man climbed out of the front passenger seat. He was obviously an American, judging by the Def Leppard tee-shirt he wore. Charity angled toward the cab, picking up her pace.

The man was athletically handsome, Charity noticed as she got closer. His tan rivaled her own, and he moved with methodical intent, seeming completely sure of who he was and what he was doing. He paid the driver, waving off the change, and turned toward Charity and the boat slips.

The cab driver looked at Charity questioningly, and she waved to let him know she needed a ride. The tall man strode toward her, nodding his head as he passed, his eyes masked by a pair of dark blue wrap-around sunglasses like some fishing guides wore.

Charity nodded back at the man and continued toward the cab. The scent of his aftershave or cologne wafted back toward her on the breeze.

"Can you take me to the Westin?" she asked the driver.

"Course I can," he replied with a gap-toothed grin.

Charity walked around and opened the front passenger door, looking toward the slips where the man had been heading. He was nowhere to be seen. Like a ghost, he'd been swallowed up by the wind and carried away. Getting into the car, she found that his scent lingered, mixed with the pungent smell of ganja that seemed to permeate the fabric inside the car.

Minutes later, the cab pulled under the portico of the Westin, and Charity got out. She paid the driver and also refused the change. A man she'd worked with a few times had mentioned how beneficial it was to stay in good graces with cab drivers. Jesse McDermitt was a retired Marine, and was sometimes hired to transport field operatives for Director Stockwell's group. He'd mentioned more than once how cab drivers and bartenders were always good sources for local information, as many people barely noticed them when talking to others.

Inside, she asked about the Casa Havana at the front desk and the desk clerk instructed her to just follow the long corridor to the left. It was in the back of that wing, facing the sea.

Entering the restaurant, she spotted the director right away. He was sitting just where she'd expect him to sit: in a corner, back to the wall, with windows on either side. He wasn't looking at the scenery, though. He was staring straight at her.

Stockwell rose as Charity approached the table. "You could pass for a Latina woman any day," Stockwell said, holding out the chair next to him.

Charity sat down, somewhat uncomfortable. "Why the meeting?" she asked, deciding to get straight to the point. She feared that he might pull her off, after what happened in Mexico.

Apparently the apprehension showed on her face. "Relax," he said. "There's just been a slight change in plans. Care for a drink?"

A drink? Charity thought. *What is this about?*

"Just water," she replied, as a waiter approached the table.

Stockwell spoke to the waiter in perfect Spanish, with a slight Cuban accent. He ordered the broiled lobster for both of them.

"I didn't know you were bilingual," Charity said after the waiter filled her water glass and left.

"A little French and German, too," he replied. Then, without any preamble, he said, "I'm afraid we're going to have to move up the timetable."

"By how much?"

"I need you in Trinidad in two days."

"I thought the best cover would be the boat," Charity said, unsure of things.

"It is," Stockwell replied. "But, on occasion, we may need to move you into position faster than that old boat can go."

"Flying commercial leaves an easy-to-follow paper trail, Director."

"You won't be flying commercial," Stockwell began. "I had your chopper moved to Gitmo and had auxiliary fuel cells installed, giving it a range of over five hundred nautical miles. It's also been renumbered. The paper trail on it will lead back to a shell company. One of the subsidiaries of that shell company is a tropical vacation magazine. You'll be posing as a travel photographer. A Navy bird will meet the Coast Guard patrol boat *Key Biscayne* twenty-five miles north of here at oh eight hundred. You'll be on the patrol boat, which leaves the port at oh six hundred. When you fly out of Gitmo, you'll have to make three fuel stops before reaching Trinidad."

CHAPTER EIGHT:

Standing on the porch, Leon listened to the sounds coming from the jungle surrounding the compound. The sun was below the treetops, shadows stretching out across the wide clearing. Though he'd grown up here and knew all the noises of the jungle, occasionally there would be something new, some strange cry in the night.

What he was now hearing were the normal jungle noises. Still, Leon felt uneasy, as if some unseen thing had been following him and watching him all day. From the water's edge a hundred meters to his right, he heard a splash in the shallows and looked that way. He had told the old man to be here at sunset; maybe the splash was him.

When Leon moved his eyes back across the darkening courtyard to his left, they fell on the old shaman now standing only a few meters away.

"Where the hell did you come from?"

The old man shrugged. "The river," he replied in English.

Leon studied Vicente Navarro closely. His head was wrapped in a red bandana, and his face was lined with jagged black lines. But it was the shaman's eyes that drew Leon's attention. They were dark and cloudy, as if a smoky fog swirled from within.

Leon visibly shook off whatever effect the old man's countenance had on him. "How did you get into the compound without anyone noticing?"

Again, the old man shrugged his shoulders and jerked a thumb behind him. "I walked," was all he said.

"Well, it is good you did not keep the babo waiting," Leon said, as he turned toward the door. "Follow me and wipe your feet off on the rug."

Leon did not like this old man. In fact, he did not like any of the native people in the area. He considered them to be only slightly above the animals that dwelled in the jungle.

Vicente mounted the steps soundlessly, following Leon into the large house. He paused and wiped the bottoms of his bare feet on the rug at the door.

Leon moved into the large foyer and pointed to a room on the right. "Wait in there. The babo will be here in a moment."

Without a word, Vicente turned and entered the high-ceilinged room off the foyer. The fact that the room was much larger than his whole house, and twice as tall, made no impression on the shaman, good or bad. One long wall was lined from floor to ceiling with leather bound books. A ladder was fixed to a track, to allow someone to reach the higher shelves.

Vicente moved quietly around the room. His eyes picked up on everything. In the center of the room, the wood floor was covered with an oval rug, the design and color of which Vicente had only seen once before, in the captain's cabin aboard a freighter on which Vicente had once sailed.

Unlike most of the indigenous people in the area, Vicente was fairly well educated in the ways of the outside world. He'd left the jungle as a young man, sailed all over the Caribbean and up and down the coasts of North and South America. He'd learned to read and write, how to reason and solve math problems. After many years aboard cargo ships, he'd returned to his jungle home, his face already lined with years and his hair graying. As a child, Vicente had learned the ancient ways of the buyei. His father had been a shaman of the boat people, as had his father before him. Vicente had saved his wages, earned from long days and longer nights at sea, and bought land along the shore of the Manamo, not far from the village where he'd been born. He'd heard about the white people of this settlement, but was drawn to his piece of land just the same. So, he'd settled into a new life as a farmer.

Walking slowly along the shelves of books, he noticed that quite a few were the same classics that he'd learned to read with. The shelves were sorted by author, it seemed. He reached for a heavy-looking volume he'd read many times.

"Do not touch that," a voice said from behind him.

Vicente turned to face the man who had spoken. He was a striking figure with brown hair. His sharp blue eyes held Vicente's, and in them the older man could see the evil boiling. He wore black trousers and an immaculate white linen shirt, open at the collar. Aside from the evil Vicente could see in his eyes, he looked a lot like the captain of the ship Vicente had sailed on as a younger man.

"Those are called books," the babo said, as if explaining a difficult subject to a small child.

Vicente gave his typical shrug and nodded toward the volume he'd been reaching for. "This one is the story of my life as a young man."

Babo slowly approached the old man and glanced at the Melville novel. "The story of your life? You are an old farmer with no knowledge of such things."

Vicente smiled slightly. "Call me Ishmael. Some years ago, never mind how long precisely, having little or no money in my purse, and nothing particular to interest me onshore, I thought I would sail about a little and see the watery part of the world." He smiled a bit more. "I too went out into the world on a ship, Babo. I know many things."

"My name is Beisch, Martin Beisch," the younger man said, surprised at the revelation that the old man could even read. "Your people call me Babo, so I assume you know who I am."

"Yes," Vicente replied. "I know who you are."

"Then you probably know that I can have my men kill you and feed you to the *caribes*."

"Yes," Vicente said. "But you will not do that."

"And why the hell do you think I will not?"

"I have been told by the light spirit that I will live to be a much older man. The why, I have no way of knowing."

Beisch studied the old man's face, then looked down at the way he was dressed: barefoot, wearing only the traditional loin cover of the Ye'kuana and a faded tie-dyed tee-shirt. The shirt was completely at odds with the rest of him, but seemed to suit him nonetheless.

"If you are such an intelligent man," the babo began, "why is it you are nothing more than a peasant farmer?"

"All men may choose what they do in life," Vicente replied, with another shrug of his shoulders. "I first chose a life at sea. Now I have chosen to work the land and help the people."

"If you want to help your people? Then grow what I tell you to grow," Beisch said. "If you do not, I will kill one of them every week. One of the younger workers."

Vicente stared into the babo's eyes. He felt no fear for himself, since the same light spirit that had visited him yesterday had returned only hours ago. She'd told him that he would win the encounter with the *itoto* of the forest people. He had only to wait and do as they asked. Vicente knew that the Mother of the Forest would send the light spirit again soon.

He also knew that the babo would carry out his threat against the people.

"Yes," Vicente said. "We will grow the coca. But, it would be a waste to cut down the cassava so close to harvest."

"A waste?"

"In both time and money," Vicente replied. "Our crops flourish. They will bring a good price in about a week. But we have no coca seed."

Beisch smiled. He'd thought the old man was going to be trouble and he'd have to kill him and a few others to get the rest to capitulate. "I can get you the seed," he said.

"Enough to plant two hundred morgen?" Vicente asked, again surprising Beisch. The morgen was the standard unit of land measure in the Old World of Beisch's ancestors. Vicente's and Anders's farms were about two and a half square kilometers in size, all prime and fertile land.

"I can have the seed delivered in five days," Beisch said, thinking this was too easy.

"We will plant the coca in seven days," Vicente said. "By then, all the cassava will be harvested. This way, when the other farmers have already harvested their coca plants, we will have a crop still growing. The season will be a long one." Then, knowing what truly drove the babo, Vicente added, "A later crop will bring more money, will it not?"

Thinking that the old man had dollar signs in his eyes and greed in his mind, Beisch nodded. "I think Leon was wrong about you. Yes, it will bring more money, but only if the monsoon floods do not wipe it all away."

"The flood waters will hold off," Vicente said. "The coca will be harvested many days before the first rains."

"Just how do you know this?" Beisch asked, cynically.

Vicente shrugged. "I am a buyei. The Forest Mother tells me these things."

"The Forest Mother, huh? Here is something you can tell her: if the coca is wiped out by the monsoons, you, Anders, his family, and all your workers will be cut and thrown into the water."

"The rain will hold," Vicente replied with conviction.

"It better, old man. Two hundred morgen of coca leaves will bring a lot of money."

There it was again. The greed of the man was easy for Vicente to manipulate. "Yes, even more so later in the season. Miguel and I will want a better price than the others because of that."

The babo smiled. To Vicente, it was like looking at the grin of the jaguar. "Yes," Beisch said, "I think that can be arranged. But you have to keep the village elders and the other farmers in line. Do you understand?"

"They will not be a problem," Vicente said, mustering what he thought was an equally evil grin. "I am the buyei. They will do as I say."

CHAPTER NINE:

Thurman Napier was at the commercial dock the next morning, as Stockwell had instructed him. A container ship was tied off, the giant cranes making easy work of the many steel containers arriving from manufacturers all over the world.

Napier went to the dock master's office and waited in line with several truck drivers, roustabouts, and a handful of businessmen. After waiting half an hour, he was told that his container was near the bottom of the ship's cargo hold and that he should come back at noon. He was also told that he'd need to provide his own truck and chassis trailer, because the yard trucks weren't permitted to go into the mountains beyond Arima.

"Where the hell am I supposed to get a truck and driver?" Thurman grumbled, realizing the Colonel had played him. If the container was on the bottom, it had to have been loaded long before the Colonel came here. "I was told transportation was arranged," he added, fixing the clerk with a fierce one-eyed stare.

The dock clerk nodded toward several men sitting and standing around a table playing cards. "Those men are drivers. I cannot vouch for any of them, or their trucks."

"Fuckin' great," Napier muttered, turning away from the counter and walking toward the table.

"Which one of you guys has the best truck and trailer?" Napier asked, as he stepped up behind two of the card players.

A man seated with his back to Napier replied without looking up from his cards. "Go 'way, mon. We all got loads, and just waitin'."

Napier stared down at the back of the man's head, guessing him to be in his early twenties and under two hundred pounds—probably way under, but two hundred was where Napier drew the line. Above that, he might have to use a little finesse. Below that, they were a mere nuisance, no different than swatting a mosquito.

With one hand, Napier grabbed the smaller man by the collar and hoisted him to his feet. The man kicked and twisted in Napier's grasp. Though Napier didn't recognize the man, he was well known in the places men like these frequented, and the smaller man knew immediately who was holding him and quit squirming.

Pointing across the table, the smaller man said, "Enrique's truck is only ten years old."

The man he'd singled out looked up and nodded his head at Napier. "It is true. Mine is the newest, but I already have a load. It's being placed on my chassis right now."

"I got a container that needs to go up to my place in the Northern Range," Napier said, lowering the first man back into his chair. "But it won't be off the ship until after lunch."

Enrique tossed his cards on the table and stood up slowly. He knew who the one-eyed man was as well. "This container is only going a short distance. I can be back by noon. To the Range, it will be two hundred dollars, half up front."

Napier scrutinized the man. He'd seen him somewhere before, he was sure. Taller than most, but still a head shorter than Napier himself. Loose-jointed and gangly, he reminded Napier of a vulture.

"One-fifty," Napier countered. "And I'll pay it all upfront, 'cause I know I can find you if you stiff me."

To Napier's surprise, Enrique countered back. "One-eighty, but I will take only half until your cargo is delivered undamaged. And if you like, we can tell the dock master, so you will not have to wait around, Mister Napier."

Thurman smiled. The man knew who he was, and so knew that money wasn't real high on his list of importance. The negotiating was merely a tradition. Sticking his hand out, Napier said, "You got a deal, Enrique."

The two shook hands and spoke quickly to the clerk, who had them each sign a release and consignment form. Napier took a page from a sketch pad he always carried. Using the pencil he kept stuck behind his ear, secured in place by the eye patch, he wrote the address and his phone number on the page and handed it to the truck driver.

"You know where this is?"

Enrique took the paper and looked at it. "Yes, I know where this is. It once belonged to di Whyte family."

"Yeah, I bought it from the old man about fifteen years ago. Call me when you're on the way, or if there's any delay."

The two men walked out of the office together. "That's my truck," Enrique said, pointing to where a container was being lowered onto a trailer chassis. "I'll be back here in two hours, well before noon. What is in the container, is it legal?"

Napier took a money roll from his pocket and peeled the bills off, handing them to Enrique. "It's legal, no worries about that. Now, don't let me down," he growled, then turned and walked down the steps to his pickup truck.

———————◆◆◆———————

Six hours later, with the sun already heading toward the summit of El Cerro del Aripo to the west, Napier heard the distinctive sound of a big truck coming up the long steep grade to his property. Enrique had called an hour earlier to say he was on the way.

Thurman had been working all day on an old Caterpillar front-end loader. It was plenty big enough to lift the container off the trailer chassis. He didn't know what the weight of the whole thing would be, but he figured if he could get the bucket's big teeth under the container, he could run chains from the top of the bucket to the far side to be able to lift it off the chassis.

Ten minutes later, just as Napier started the behemoth, Enrique's truck came around the last turn and through the gate. He maneuvered his truck into position right in front of the loader, which Napier was glad to see. The hydraulics for the steering leaked terribly.

"The invoice says the container stays," Enrique said, as he climbed out of the cab.

"You got any real big chains?" Thurman asked. "At least twenty feet long?"

Enrique looked at the loader and then at the thirty-five-foot container. "I see what you want to do. Yes, I have chains. The weight is just over twelve thousand pounds. Two of my big chains will work."

Napier moved the loader into position, slightly lifting the side of the container, with the teeth under it and the top of the bucket against the side. Enrique climbed up to the top of the container and reached down to attach the ends of the chains to two hooks welded on top of the bucket. After dropping the other ends of the chains over the far side, he scrambled down and hooked them through the pockets at the two corners, pulling all the slack out and hooking the chains back onto themselves.

When Enrique came around the front of the truck, he circled a finger in the air, signaling Napier to lift. The old Caterpillar strained against the chains as air pressure began hissing from the overcharged airbags of the trailer's suspension. Suddenly the big container popped free, rocking the loader but remaining steady.

Napier backed up enough to clear the trailer chassis and slowly eased the steel box to the ground. He hadn't counted on keeping the big steel box, but his mind was already thinking of how he could use it. Maybe bury it and turn it into an emergency shelter.

Opening the door, Napier looked inside and let out a low whistle. The boat sat on an aluminum trailer, both obviously brand new. He went inside and saw that the boat was strapped securely to the trailer, which was in turn chained to the floor. It didn't look like it had moved, and there was no apparent damage.

Outside, Napier paid Enrique the balance, along with a twenty-dollar tip, and after helping him retrieve his chains, sent him on his way. It took another thirty minutes to remove the chains and blocks holding the boat trailer in place. He used the blocks as steps to allow him to back his pickup into the container and hook up the trailer.

Working quickly so nobody would see—not that there was anyone looking—Napier moved the boat straight to the big hangar adjacent to his house. Old man Whyte had been a flyer many years ago, taking people and small loads from island to island, and adventure fishermen up the Manamo River. He'd owned a small amphibian airplane, which he'd kept in the hangar.

Once Napier had the boat in place, he unhitched it and began inspecting it closely. Though it was nearly thirty feet in length, he was able to lift the tongue of the trailer and move it around fairly easily, a good testament to its light weight.

The boat was set up as a center console, with minimal controls. The hull and console were painted flat black. The deck was a lattice-style hardwood, raised above the bilges on either side of the console. It looked sturdy and capable enough.

Not a true tunnel hull, more like a catamaran, Thurman thought as he peered under the boat from the bow.

Aft the console, the gunwales flared on the inside, leaving only a few feet of room between them at the transom. On top of each of these wide spots were large lockable hatch covers. He opened one of them and let out another low whistle. Nestled in the confines of the gunwale was a huge V-twin engine. It looked similar to a motorcycle engine, but much larger than any he'd ever seen on a bike. Cooling fins on the cylinder and head told Napier that it was an air-cooled engine. Aft of the hatch cover on both sides were two large air outlets, also painted black.

"Where the hell does the air come from?" Thurman asked out loud, looking for similar intakes facing forward. Not seeing any, he climbed up into the boat and looked around. Sticking his head down inside the engine compartment, he saw what looked like a six-inch tube going forward, inside the gunwale. Moving forward, he found the intakes. Mounted just aft the bow, up under the gunwale, were two oil coolers, also painted black. Each one had its own large electric fan behind it.

Going back to the console, he turned the two keys to the on position and heard both fans engage. Reaching a hand out, he felt a good bit of air blowing up out of the engine bay. Closing the hatch, he pushed the button below the first key and the port engine roared to life.

Noticing a large envelope tucked between the throttles, Napier shut off the engine and opened the flap on the envelope. Inside were the maintenance and operating manuals. He sat down at the helm seat and began reading.

CHAPTER
TEN:

Before the sun had even tinged the eastern sky, Charity was getting into the same cab that she'd taken to and from the Westin the day before. Upon returning to the marina, she paid for a month of slip rental, telling the man at the marina office that she had an emergency back home and would be flying out.

The man promised that he'd have someone check her boat daily, to make sure the bilge pumps were working and everything remained in order.

Charity spent the rest of the day packing everything she thought she'd need into a black nylon backpack, before turning in early to be rested for the next day.

The cab dropped her off at the commercial shipping pier, where she easily found *Key Biscayne*. Approaching the gangway, a man wearing a Coast Guard ensign's bars stood waiting.

"Abigail Suerto?" he asked, as Charity walked toward him wearing black jeans and a long-sleeved black work shirt.

"Yes, Ensign," Charity replied. "I understand *Key Biscayne* will be taking me to a rendezvous?"

"Yes, ma'am," the young man replied. "And we're under orders from Homeland Security not to ask you anything. I'm Ensign John Taylor."

"Thank you, Ensign Taylor." Charity wondered what the rest of the crew thought about having an obvious spook on board, especially a woman. "I'll prefer to be on the bridge, if that's all right with the captain."

"He's already asked that you join him there, ma'am. Please follow me."

The two made their way to the ship's bridge, where Ensign Taylor introduced Charity to Lieutenant Spears. After shaking her hand, Spears turned to the ensign. "Give the orders to cast off, John."

"Aye, sir," Ensign Taylor replied and began giving orders over the ship's intercom.

As Charity watched from the bridge, the crew quickly loosed the ship from the dock. "Take her out, XO," Spears said to Taylor.

The executive officer spoke into the loudspeaker microphone, "Underway! Shift colors!"

Taylor began giving orders to the helmsman as Spears turned to Charity. "Join me for coffee, Miss Suerto?"

"The Coast Guard is notorious for having good coffee," Charity replied. "I'd love some."

Charity followed Spears down to the ship's galley. "Cream or sugar?" he asked, pouring a mug.

"No thanks," she replied, feeling the ship shudder for a moment and then start moving forward.

Spears handed her the mug and poured a second one for himself. "I'm under orders not to ask you any questions. But I think we've met before, haven't we?"

Charity studied the man's face. She knew the *Key Biscayne* was home ported in Key West, but she'd rarely gone down there.

No, she thought. *I've never seen this guy before.*

"It's possible," she said. "Have you ever been to Southern California?"

"No, I can't say as I have," Spears replied. "So, what's a SoCal girl going to Gitmo for?"

Charity took a slow sip from her coffee as she stared into the man's eyes. Finally, she placed the mug in the sink, coffee half-finished. "That's a question you were ordered not to ask," she said.

"Look," Spears began, "this is my boat. I've been ordered to sail north from here. Cuba is north from here. And you look more Cuban than Californian. I just want to know what I'm sailing my vessel and crew toward."

Charity considered it a moment. Tensions between the US and Cuban governments had been on the rise lately. Perhaps that really was his only concern.

"Just for the record," Charity said, looking intently into the man's eyes, "where I'm going and what I'm doing have nothing to do with Cuba, aside from stopping in Guantanamo Bay for about ten minutes. I just need to be somewhere, faster than my boat can get me there. Nothing more. Even that's way more than you should know. Both for my benefit and your own."

Spears looked at his watch. "We'll be on station in about an hour. I'd appreciate it if you remained on the bridge."

"Fair enough," Charity said, and followed him back up to the bridge.

The ship was moving north in the sound at what Charity judged to be about ten knots. She stood quietly with Spears at the back of the bridge area, as the XO expertly guided the helmsman out of the sound.

"Make your course zero degrees, helm," Taylor said. "Increase speed to twenty-five knots."

"Zero degrees, twenty-five knots," the petty officer at the helm responded. "Aye aye, sir."

The ship shuddered again and began to accelerate, just as the sun was beginning to peek over a cloudless eastern sky.

"The *Key Biscayne* is a patrol boat," Spears explained, as the small ship quickly accelerated. "She doesn't have a helo-pad like a cutter. When the Navy chopper arrives, they can lower a cable with a basket or horse-collar to take you up. Your choice."

"Not a problem," Charity said. "I've gotten off boats in worse ways. The collar is fine."

Spears looked over at her, a puzzled look on his face. He was about to say something, when the radio operator turned around. "Incoming voice-comm from the Navy helo, sir."

"Put it on speaker," Spears replied.

The radioman flipped a switch, then spoke into the mic. "Repeat your last, Frogman."

"We're eighty miles out and closing, *Key Biscayne*. Understand you have a priority package to be picked up."

Spears stepped up beside the radioman and picked up the microphone. "Frogman, this is *Key Biscayne* Six Actual. We are on route and on time. A horse-collar will be fine for the package."

"Roger that, *Key Biscayne*. See you shortly."

Spears turned to Taylor and said, "John, take our guest to the fantail and get her ready."

"Aye, sir," he replied and turned to Charity. "Follow me, please, Miss Suerto."

Taylor led the way down to the deck and back to the stern of the ship. The seas were calm, just an occasional roller from the east that caused the deck to tilt side-to-side as they passed under.

Charity removed her backpack and placed it on the deck. From one of the pockets, she removed a black ball cap with DHS printed across the front in large white letters. She quickly twirled her hair up into a small bun, fixing it in place with a single bobby pin. She pulled the hat on tight and checked the pack to make sure the pockets were all secured, then removed a six-foot-long tether from a zippered pouch between the straps.

The sound of the approaching chopper could be heard above the wind. Charity scanned the sky, hooking the tether firmly around her waist, just above her belt.

Taylor pointed slightly to starboard. "There it is."

Within minutes, the helicopter circled and came up from the stern. A door on the side opened and someone reached out to hook a thick yellow collar to the winch cable.

"I appreciate the lift, John," Charity said. "Tell the skipper I said thanks for the coffee."

Taylor extended his hand. "Best of luck, Miss Suerto."

Charity shook his hand, as the wash from the chopper rotors buffeted them. The man at the door lowered the cable, and Taylor let it drop completely until the cable made contact with the steel deck, to discharge any static electricity, before picking up the collar, helping Charity get it fitted snuggly around her back and under both arms. Then he stepped away from her and signaled the chopper to begin hoisting.

The cable tightened and Charity was lifted from the deck, spinning slowly. The tether of her pack pulled tight as it came off the deck, and the pilot moved the bird out over water. The tether pulled down on her pants slightly, causing her shirt tail to come out. The rotor wash tugged at the tail of her shirt, like a flag on a windy day, exposing her belly and hips.

Seconds later, the man in the door reached out and grabbed her hand, pulling her toward the door. Once inside, he pulled her pack up and disconnected the winch cable from her harness.

"Welcome aboard, ma'am," he said. Charity saw that he wore seaman chevrons on his flight suit. He pointed toward a pair of forward-facing jump seats, and the two quickly strapped in.

"Thanks, Seaman," Charity mouthed over the scream of the engine, as the chopper began to climb and accelerate to the east. The seaman handed her a headset and she put it on, adjusting the boom mic so it barely touched her lips.

"We'll arrive at Gitmo in about an hour, ma'am," a voice said. "I'm Lieutenant Perry Bradshaw, my co-pilot is Lieutenant Milt Percy. That's Seaman Wayne Chaffey, you already met."

"I'm Special Agent Suerto," Charity said. "Thanks for the lift."

"Like I said, it'll be about an hour, so relax as best you can. I personally did a preflight inspection on your bird, an hour before we left. She had a leak in one of the turbine's oil lines. It wasn't much, more of a weep than a leak. Wayne took care of it."

Charity smiled at the young man seated next to her. "Thank you, Wayne. You're also a turbine mechanic?"

"Budget cuts, ma'am," he replied with a wink. "A lot of us at Gitmo have more than one specialty. That's some chopper you have. If I didn't know better, I'd never have guessed it wasn't converted to a civilian aircraft."

CHAPTER ELEVEN:

Paddling through the darkness was nothing new for Vicente. As a *nibora* of but six years, he'd helped his father build his own *bongo*. In his adolescence, he'd been on many hunting parties, traveling in his own boat with the older men.

The bright stars in the sky illuminated the Manamo and guided him, his boat slipping silently through the water. Along the banks, Vicente could hear the night sounds of the jungle. The river and forest were both dangerous places, especially at night.

In the water, the caribe waited. He'd learned in his younger days that the caribe was not only the largest of the many piranha species but, pound for pound, had the most powerful bite of any animal in the world. Even before he left the jungle, he'd known their danger.

In addition to the piranha, large snakes and crocodiles were also common in the water. There were eels that could shock a small child into paralysis, and even large sharks were sometimes known to come far up the fresh-water river in search of food. Vicente had learned of these sharks while at sea, as well. They were called bull sharks, one of the most aggressive sharks in the world.

At the water's edge was where the anaconda, caiman, and crocodile lay in wait for unwary river visitors. Further into the jungle, there were poisonous snakes, frogs, spiders, centipedes, even ants. But it was the jaguar that was most dangerous. A single swipe from one of the great cat's paws could eviscerate a grown man, and its bite could crush a man's skull.

When Vicente arrived at the spit that marked the boundary between his and Miguel's properties, he turned into the shallow cove, avoiding the spot where his other boat lay broken on the bottom. There were a number of other canoes of various shapes and sizes pulled up onto the bank, and a young man stood waiting.

"The elders are all here, Buyei," the *nibora* said, holding Vicente's boat, so he could step out.

Without another word, the young man pulled the canoe up onto the bank, as Vicente started up the path toward his house. The elders from the villages upriver were an eclectic group. Many had taken to dressing in clothes from America, some embracing the new ways, like a cult. All of them were old men, by jungle standards—some in their fifties and sixties—but most were compar-atively younger men, still old in the ways of the jungle.

Vicente's cook fire was going as he approached. Miguel and another younger man rose and came toward him. "We feared you would never return from the *itoto* village," Miguel said.

"Did I not say that I would?"

"Yes, Buyei," Miguel replied. "But they are evil people. I was worried."

"No need, my friend," Vicente said, as they reached the fire.

The old man walked around the circle of men sitting at the fire, laying his hand lightly on the shoulder of each of them, before taking the position of honor at the top of the circle.

Looking around the fire, Vicente made eye contact with each of the elders. These men represented numerous tribal communities all up and down the river. They were mostly from the Ye'kuana, Warao, and Yanomamo people, but several smaller sects were also represented.

"We will smoke first," Vicente said, pulling his little pack closer to him.

"What happened?" one of the younger men impatiently asked the old shaman. "Did you speak to the babo?"

Seated next to Vicente, Guyan Montenegro fixed the younger man with a cold hard stare. "The buyei said we will smoke first," the older man cautioned. "Not all of our ways are to be corrupted by the outsiders."

Vicente withdrew his pipe and placed it across his bare knees. Opening the small pouch, he filled the bowl of the pipe with the dried and crushed yopo seed. Lighting it with a twig from the fire, Vicente drew deeply, then washed the smoke from the bowl back across his head and passed it to his left.

As the pipe went around the small group gathered around the fire, Vicente watched each one practice the ancient ritual. When Guyan finally returned the pipe to Vicente, he again placed it across his knees and looked around the fire at each man.

"When our cassava are harvested," Vicente began, "Miguel and I will plant the coca seed."

Each man's face turned slowly toward the fire. Those that were farmers had been cowed by the *itoto* and were already growing the valuable cash crop. Those that had once done other jobs now worked for the babo in one way or another. Learning that even the old shaman's magic was powerless against the interlopers was tragic news. They had all hoped that Vicente and Miguel holding out might turn the tide.

The white people had been here since before most of the elders had been born, but the people of the forest had been here for all time. The whites had mostly kept to themselves on the great island. Their only interaction with the forest people for two generations had been their mining operations in the mountains—and, before that, cutting the timber.

"But the coca we grow will never be harvested," Vicente added. "The days of the *itoto* grow few."

Guyan was the first to speak. "How can we fight them?"

Again, all eyes were back on Vicente. "We will not fight them. Not yet, anyway. I have told Miguel about a visit I had here yesterday. The Forest Mother has had enough of the *itoto's* ways. She sent a spirit to me, here to this very place. The spirit appeared in all ways as if she were one of the people, except she was much taller than even the tallest man. I sense that she is a great warrior spirit of some kind, but it was not clear. Her hair is long and hangs over her face. Behind the hair, her eyes flash with a white light. I knew without knowing that she had been sent by the Mother of the Forest, and would seek justice for the people."

Vicente paused and ceremoniously loaded the pipe's bowl again. Before continuing, he lit it and once again passed it to the left. "This warrior spirit conveyed to me that we should do what the *itoto* tell us. When the time is right, the spirit will banish these outsiders to the netherworld, once and for all time."

Guyan again handed the pipe to Vicente. The yopo seed was beginning to take effect. Each man's face had lost the edge it had had when Vicente arrived. Guyan looked up at the smoke climbing into the dark sky. Sparks from the fire meandered up to become stars in the velvety blackness.

Still looking up, Guyan asked, "Did this spirit have a name? We should each offer thanks in our own way."

"Yes," Vicente replied. Guyan looked at his old friend and spiritual leader of the many tribes and clans. Vicente returned his gaze. "The spirit is called the dancer of the wind."

CHAPTER TWELVE:

As soon as the Navy helo touched down on the tarmac at Guantanamo Bay, Charity climbed out, arching her back and stretching. Looking around, there wasn't a whole lot to see. There was a control tower halfway down the airstrip, with a few buildings clustered along the taxiway. Aside from that, it looked like one of many palm-covered islands in the Caribbean.

Looking further inland to the north, Charity saw the mountains rising above the jungle. The jungle seemed to call out to her somehow. She shook it off, as Seaman Chaffey approached. The pilots were still in the cockpit, going through their post-flight check.

"Your bird's in the hangar," Chaffey said, pointing to one of the large buildings by the taxiway.

"Thanks, Wayne," Charity said. "Can you take me there now, or do I need to check in with someone?"

"Sure, I'll take you over. As far as anyone knows, you're not even here, so nobody to check in with."

Minutes later, the two of them stepped through the slightly open hangar door. Charity removed her sunglasses and looked around. Her Huey sat in the center of the building. It was still black, but now sported legal numbers on the tail boom, and the phony company name and logo on the doors.

It also had wheels added to the skids. Not the typical dolly wheels used to drag the chopper around, though. The skids had been lengthened and reinforced aft, and large double wheels with beefy-looking hydraulic shocks were mounted a little further back than where the dollies were usually located, near the center of gravity.

Forward, smaller caster-type wheels were mounted on both skids, to allow the bird to turn on the ground. These probably wouldn't survive a hard landing, but in the event of one, she still had the sturdy skids.

Walking toward the helo, Charity inspected the odd retrofit work. She'd never seen a Huey with wheels, but everything looked as though it had been professionally engineered and installed. They'd even installed a hydraulic system to let the bird sit on the skids when not in use.

"Where was the oil leak?" she asked.

Chaffey quickly moved a ladder next to the Huey, climbed up, and fished a Snoopy tool from his pocket. Turning the Dzus locks holding the starboard engine cover in place, he handed it down to her.

Climbing down, he said, "It was on the high pressure line from the pump to the oil cooler. It was barely a wet spot, really." Charity climbed up to inspect the engine, as Chaffey continued. "I removed the line, checked it for blockages and cracks, then replaced both seals and reinstalled it. I had the hangar guys move her outside and Lieutenant Bradshaw and I spun the blades for an hour."

Charity took a small pen light from her pocket and shined it on the pump, looking closely at the oil line connections. "I'll keep an eye on it," she said, seeing no sign of dirt or oil. "Thanks for checking her over so thoroughly."

"We don't get many overnight visitors," Chaffey said, as she climbed down. "It was a pleasurable diversion."

Charity smiled, and Chaffey climbed back up, replaced the cover and climbed back down again.

"I'll be leaving immediately. Can you have her brought outside?"

"Give me ten minutes," Chaffey said, trotting off to the corner of the hangar.

Quickly climbing aboard, Charity opened the floor panel in the back of the Huey. Inside were a number of cameras and lenses in cases, along with a sturdy tripod and other equipment. She moved everything out of the way and searched the starboard bulkhead for the release catch. Though Stockwell had told her just where it was, it still took a moment to find.

The engine on the tow motor started as Charity pushed the release catch, and the edge of the storage box popped up slightly. She got a finger under the lip and lifted the box up and out of the recess, exposing the hidden compartment below it. The bottom of the box had a metal ring into which the catch fit when the box was pushed down into the recess, snapping and locking the box in place.

Inside was a new M40 rifle, scope, suppressor, ammo, and a Sig Sauer P229 handgun. Next to the rifle was a red backpack. She pulled it out, strapping it in the co-pilot's seat, and quickly put her black backpack inside.

Hearing the tow motor moving at the far end of the hangar, Charity quickly snapped the box back into place, checking the tightness of the lip, then put all the camera gear back inside. Before exiting the chopper, she pushed the release again. The box popped up, even with the added weight. She snapped it back and closed the hatch.

Climbing out, Charity walked back out through the hangar door and waited as Bradshaw and Percy approached. Halfway to where she waited by the door, the two gave each other a fist bump and the co-pilot angled off toward what Charity figured was a ready room.

"You leaving right away?" Perry Bradshaw asked, just as the large metal doors began retracting, the wheels making a rusty, squeaking sound.

"In just a few minutes," Charity replied.

Bradshaw frowned. "Percy and I were hoping you might join us for a drink in the Officer's Club later. We don't get a lot of visitors here."

"I'll have to take a raincheck on that," Charity said, flashing a disarming smile. "I have a long way to go and very little time to get there."

They watched as Chaffey pulled the helicopter out of the hangar with the tow motor, basically a four-wheeled motorized cart with a seat and steering wheel. It had a tow bar on the front connected to the front of the Huey's skids, allowing Chaffey to maneuver the Huey around. The seat on this one didn't look at all comfortable, with padding showing in some places, and just plain gone in others.

Once Chaffey had Charity's helicopter far enough away from the building, he set the brake on the machine, jumped down, and decoupled it from the chopper. Then he went around and opened the door on the pilot's side of the aircraft.

"I guess it would be pointless to ask what *Tropical Luxury Magazine* is."

Charity smiled as she put on her dark aviator sunglasses. "It's the magazine I work for," she said, extending her hand. "Gabriella Fleming, photographer."

Bradshaw shook her hand, laughing. "You be careful, *Gabriella Fleming.*"

"You do the same, Lieutenant Bradshaw," Charity said, walking toward her bird. She loved being out on the water, but felt even more at home in the air, and she'd missed flying.

Chaffey drove the tow motor out of the way, waving as he passed Charity. She did a quick walk-around inspection on the aircraft before climbing in the cockpit. Then she raised the wheels so the skids were in contact with the tarmac, and worked through her startup checklist, bringing the big turbine engine humming to life.

When she lowered the wheels again, the bird started to turn. She countered the torque with a little left pedal and, as she rotated the throttle to the full open position, she noticed the co-pilot coming out of the ready room, dressed in civilian clothes.

Charity picked the helicopter up to a hover. The center of gravity felt normal, and the flight controls were smooth and responsive. Using the foot pedals, she turned the chopper toward the taxiway. Out of the corner of her eye, Charity saw Bradshaw open his wallet, take out a bill, and hand it to Percy.

Charity grinned and pulled the trigger on the cyclic push-to-talk switch so she could call the tower. Once she got clearance, she hovered down the taxiway and brought the Huey to the center of the runway.

Charity pivoted the nose of the aircraft toward the windward end of the runway and glanced over at the hangar. All three men stood watching. In one fluid movement, she pulled up hard on the collective and pushed forward on the cyclic.

The rotors beat the air heavily, with the distinctive whumping sound of the big Huey. The tail boom came way up, pitching the chopper forward at a steep angle. Quickly, it gathered speed, rising to ten feet off the runway.

At the end of the runway, the Huey was traveling at nearly a hundred knots, as it flashed across the sand and grass, between the end of the strip and the entrance to Guantanamo Bay. Flying out over the water, Charity pulled back and to the right on the cyclic, and the bird climbed steeply, turning south over the mouth of the bay, leaving Leeward Point Field behind.

Enough showing off, Charity thought, knowing that the heavy whump-whump of the Huey's rotors during an extreme maneuver could be heard for miles. She reduced power and leveled off about a hundred feet above the water. She maintained a due south course until she was fifteen miles off the Cuban coast. Then she climbed to one thousand feet and turned east-southeast toward her first planned fuel stop in Santo Domingo.

It would be only a three-hour flight. She'd refuel there, get back in the air, and make Saint Croix three hours after that, just before dark. Aboard *Wind Dancer*, the trip would have taken four days.

Tomorrow, she planned to fly out early, refuel in Martinique, then arrive in Port of Spain, Trinidad by mid-afternoon, more than a week earlier than planned. Charity worried about the *Dancer* being left alone for at least five days, probably a week. But it did feel good to be back in the air.

CHAPTER THIRTEEN:

Thurman Napier was up before the sun, something rare these days, unless he had a serious job to do. Opening the big hangar doors in the humid tropical air just before dawn brought more than a few beads of perspiration popping out on his forehead. Once he had the door pushed open a good twelve feet, he stopped and looked at the black boat.

Within minutes, he had the trailer hooked to his pickup and pulled the boat out into the gathering daylight. There wasn't any need to close the door, so he continued out to Eastern Main Road, turned right, and headed toward the coastal town of Plum Mitan. A friend had a private boat ramp there in a small cove.

The woman that Stockwell wanted him to take upriver wouldn't be arriving until late the following day, so he had at least thirty-six hours to see what the boat could do and get familiar with how it handled.

Seas were usually rougher on the windward side of the island of Trinidad, where he was headed. Napier wanted to see how the multihull handled the chop. He had no doubt it would perform well in shallow water, but there just wasn't any between the island and the mainland.

It was a slow, time-consuming drive down the twisting mountain road, and it took over an hour to reach his friend's house. Pulling the boat into the long driveway, he saw Marc Snow working on his boat. Napier tapped his horn and Snow looked toward him.

He'd met Snow, another ex-pat like himself, in a bar. They'd hit it off right away, matching shots of cheap rum with one another until the place closed down. Neither man was really sure who helped who out of the bar that night, but they'd both awakened on the fifty-foot schooner Snow was building. He'd been working on it steadily for five years and would probably be at least another year before he launched it. Napier had offered to help, but Snow took great pride in the fact that he'd fashioned every board and turned every brass screw himself.

Stopping the truck and getting out, Napier met Snow at the bottom of the ladder.

"What in blazes is that?" Snow asked, walking toward the black boat.

"It's called a boat," Napier replied, with a chuckle. "Unlike that pile of driftwood you're working on."

"Hardy har, I guess I walked into that one.

"A buddy brought it to me. Wants me to test it out on the Manamo."

Snow looked at Napier doubtfully. "Well, if anyone's nuts enough to cross Columbus Channel in that thing, it'd be you. Where's the engines?"

Napier stepped up on the trailer's fender and levered himself into the boat. Lifting the hatch, he pointed. "Twin air-cooled vee-twins."

Snow climbed up and looked inside the engine bay, letting out a low whistle. "Vee-twins? Those things are huge. How many ponies?"

"One-eighty," Napier replied. "Each. Wanna go out with me? I need to see how she handles the chop first."

"Sure," Snow replied. "If you promise not to kill me."

"I ain't killed you yet, have I?"

"Well," Snow replied, grinning. "Not for lack of trying."

Twenty minutes later, the two men had the boat in the water and tied off to Snow's pier, the engines idling with a throaty rumble.

"You got any beer?" Snow asked.

"Cooler's in the back of the truck," Thurman replied, jerking his thumb as he climbed aboard. Marc started toward the truck and Thurman called after him: "Grab that bottle of rum off the front seat, too."

Minutes later, Napier turned the boat around the small spit of land that protected the cove and pushed the twin throttles about a third of the way forward.

The exhaust blasted and the boat surged forward, straight and level. The feeling was different than most boats he'd driven; most boats brought the bow up and clawed their way up on top of the water.

The first wave they encountered had already broken, and the boat knifed through the churning whitewater, rising only slightly out of the water. The next wave came at them, threatening to break across the bow. The boat rose up to meet the breaking wave, and the twin hulls sliced cleanly through, spray shooting forward then up and over the single bowsprit in a cat's sneeze. The console and small windshield kept the spray off the two men standing behind it.

"Not too shabby!" Snow shouted over the engines.

Thurman turned the boat and increased throttle. It responded like a sports car, remaining flat and level in the turn. With another wave approaching, Thurman angled to take it at a forty-five-degree angle.

Surprisingly, the boat crested the wave, coming slightly out of the water for a moment, before the aft quarter of the twin hulls came gently back down. No rough crash, like most boats.

Encouraged and thrilled at the performance so far, Napier pushed both throttles to the stops and headed further offshore. In seconds, the boat reached its top speed. Snow looked at the dash-mounted GPS. "Fifty knots! Holy shit!"

Slowly, Napier pulled back on the throttles until the boat settled down to idle speed, then he jammed them both to full throttle. He was certain the roar of the two engines could be heard all the way up in the mountains. The boat launched forward, like a rocket sled on rails, reaching fifty knots in just a few seconds.

When Thurman slowed again, he put the boat in neutral, then shut down the engines, leaving the cooling fans running. Mono-hull boats would rock precariously in these conditions, but the wide beam and twin hulls kept the boat a lot more stable, and moving around on the deck was much easier.

"Check the starboard engine," Napier said as he stepped over and lifted the port engine cover.

The engine bay was as dry as could be. Any water that came over the bow or gunwales drained through scuppers at the stern. In really rough conditions, some spray might get sucked through the cooling fans, but the engine bay was separated from the rest of the hull, with two bilge pumps to remove any water that got in.

"Dry as a bone," Snow said. "Oil level's fine and it's actually pretty cool to the touch."

Napier bent over, licked a finger, and touched it quickly to one of the cylinder heads. When he touched it again, it was warm, but not hot. The oil coolers probably helped a lot in dissipating the heat.

For the next two hours, Napier put the boat through a punishing sea trial and was thoroughly impressed with everything. Running it closer to shore, parallel to the breaking waves, he found that the deck area occasionally filled ankle-deep with water and foam, but it drained out quickly and had almost no effect on the boat's stability and handling. One unusually large wave caught Thurman off guard and pushed the boat a lot closer to shore than he wanted to run.

"Turn out!" Snow shouted, grabbing the rail mounted to his side of the console with both hands. He fully expected the boat to run aground at any second and come to a lurching halt.

Napier jammed the throttles, racing ahead of the breaking wave in no more than half a foot of water. Ahead of the foamy break, he finally turned, cresting the wave at a tight angle. The boat shot up, the port side coming up higher than the starboard. The boat settled back into the water smoothly.

"That was insane!" Napier shouted, his heart pounding with adrenaline.

"That hadda pick up a ton of sand, man," Snow said, as Thurman slowed and stopped the boat a hundred yards off the beach.

"Check the intakes," Napier said, again opening the port hatch on his side. The huge water jet was directly behind the engine. Checking the intake strainer, he found only a few grains of sand.

"Almost nothin'," Snow commented. "How big are the intake ports under the hull?"

"Hell if I know."

"You never checked?"

Thurman closed and latched the cover. "Didn't see a need to, but now I'm curious. That couldn't have been no more than six inches of water."

"Six my ass," Snow said, laughing and peeling off his tee-shirt. He dumped the contents of his pants pockets onto the dash. "On this side, you were riding on nothin' but foam, buddy."

Snow put one hand on the gunwale and vaulted over the side, splashing into the water. He took a deep breath and dove under the boat, surfacing a moment later.

"Can't see real clear without a mask, but they're really long and narrow, covered with some kind of mesh."

Napier reached down and grabbed Snow's arm, nearly pulling him out of the water without any help. "Don't know much about jet drives," he admitted. "Tunnel hulls, sure. What kind of mesh?"

"Got me," Snow replied. "I've seen a lot of jet drives, but nothing with this kind of intake. I guess with the really big area, the mesh helps keep debris out, without sacrificing how much water can enter."

Hours later, the gas tank was sucking fumes and the cooler was long empty. The two men idled back into the cove, surfing just ahead of a wave. The sun was nearing the mountain peaks as they tied off to the dock. Napier tilted the rum bottle to his lips, then tossed the empty up on shore.

"You wanna get it out of the water?" Snow asked.

"Nah, it can wait till morning. I was gonna run her harder tomorrow, but I don't think that's possible."

"Won't argue with you there," Snow said. "Let's go into town and blow off some steam."

CHAPTER FOURTEEN:

It was early afternoon when Charity brought her helicopter down on the tarmac at Piarco International Airport, ten miles east of Port of Spain. She had a room reserved at a nearby hotel, where she planned to rest up. In the morning, she was going to fly up to the home of the man she was supposed to meet. He had a small airstrip and a hangar there.

Before leaving her last fuel stop on Martinique, Charity sent a message to her handler, asking for more information on the man she'd be meeting. The saved reply contained an attachment, which she would open once she was in the hotel room. If the man was as trustworthy as Stockwell had said, she'd have him fly up the river with her to have a look around.

After securing the bird and checking in with Customs, Charity walked out the front door of the private aviation building and looked around. The small parking lot held a handful of cars, but no cabs. Off to the right, she saw a covered area with benches in front of the general aviation building. A lone taxi sat parked in the shade of the overhanging awning, its right tires up on the sidewalk; Charity assumed this was to get the car out of the direct sunlight. She walked toward the cab, her backpack and computer bag over one shoulder, and her small flight bag in her hand.

"Where to, Miss?" the cab driver asked as Charity approached.

"The Hyatt," Charity replied, tossing her gear in the backseat and climbing in after it.

"Yes, Miss," The driver replied, starting the engine. "No plane s'posed to be in for another hour. Did you come in on dat helicopter?"

Charity opened a side pouch of her backpack and searched around inside with her hand. Zipping it closed, she checked the middle pouch and found the flat metal business card holder Stockwell said would be in it.

"Yes," she said, handing a card to the driver and calling to mind what McDermitt had told her about cab drivers. "I'm a photographer and pilot with *Tropical Luxury Magazine*."

"You di pilot *and* di photographer?"

"It allows me to visit beautiful places on my own and get paid for it," Charity replied, noting the man's name on the permit mounted to the dash. "I'm doing a multi-page layout on Trinidad, Devin—but mostly as a jumping-off point for anglers on the Manamo River."

The cab bounced off the curb, the driver taking lefts and rights out to the main road. There, he pulled out onto Churchill Roosevelt Highway, headed west toward the coast. "Fishing on dat river? Yuh might catch piranha, not sure what else dere is."

Ten minutes later, the cab pulled up to the hotel. Charity gave the driver a decent tip and walked inside. She breezed through the check-in process and was in her room just minutes later.

Powering up her laptop, she carried it out onto the balcony, to acquire a better satellite signal. A small table and two chairs were set up, facing the water. The view was magnificent, the water stretching out to the horizon.

For just a moment, Charity felt cheated. Two chairs, a romantic view—they probably even had a hot tub in the bathroom. A place for vacationing couples. She quickly pushed the thought aside and sat down, clicking the desktop icon to connect with the satellite.

Once the saved file was downloaded, Charity opened it and began reading about Thurman Napier. She scanned the ten-page dossier, picking out the high points of the man's past. He'd enlisted in the Army at age seventeen and was sent to Vietnam for his senior trip. At nineteen, he was sent there a second time, attached to the Army's vaunted 101st Airborne Division.

As she scanned the document, a name caught her eye. A young lieutenant by the name of Travis Stockwell had recommended Napier for a Silver Star medal. Their unit had been nearly overrun by the enemy. Napier was a sergeant and, although wounded twice, he continued to direct his men, often charging from one position to another through a hail of small arms fire. He'd been shot and thought killed twice, but only lost consciousness for a minute or two before springing back up and engaging the enemy once more.

Connections made in combat sometimes last a lifetime, Charity thought.

As evening approached, she called down to find out where the restaurant was located. The desk clerk told her she had several choices, including the rooftop pool bar, which served lighter fare.

Before leaving her room, Charity changed into a swimsuit, wrapping a colorful sarong around her waist. A few laps in the pool might help her unwind. She also called the number Stockwell had given her for Thurman Napier.

"Yeah," a gruff sounding voice replied after three rings.

"Mister Napier, my name is Gabby Fleming. A mutual friend gave me your number."

"I ain't got any friends, lady," Napier replied with a low moan. "What do you want?"

"The friend's name is Travis," Charity said. There was silence on the other end. "Are you still there?" she asked. "The friend's name is…"

"Yeah, I heard ya," Napier interrupted, with a groan. "Are you on the island?"

"Yes, I'm staying at the Hyatt. I'd like to fly upriver in the morning. Are you available as a guide?"

The man laughed. "A guide, you say? You planning some kinda half-assed fishing expedition?"

"Something like that," Charity replied. "Look, I want to do just a basic fly-by, no stops. It'd be a big help, if I knew what it was I was flying over. I can pay you extra."

Napier laughed again, followed by another moan. "Look, lady, I don't need your money. Right now, you're interrupting a pretty decent blowjob, though. Where ya want me to meet you in the morning?"

Ugh, Charity thought. *Way too much information.*

"Give me the GPS numbers where your house is located. I was told you had an airstrip."

Charity wrote the numbers down, as Napier gave them to her. He ended the call with a low moan and Charity had a sudden urge to wash her phone with industrial-strength disinfectant.

When she got to the rooftop pool and bar, she gave up on any notion of swimming; the pool was full of rowdy teenagers. Instead, she took a seat at a table in the corner of the rooftop terrace, overlooking the Gulf of Paria.

A waiter brought her a glass of water almost instantly, taking her drink order and leaving a menu.

"I've seen you before," a man said, from the next table.

She looked over her menu at him. He was obviously American, but without any discernable regional accent. She recognized him immediately. She'd seen him at the marina on Grand Cayman, as she was getting into the cab to meet Stockwell. Her senses went on full alert, though outwardly she only smiled.

"Three days ago on Grand Cayman," Charity replied, a slight Cuban accent to her voice. From behind her dark sunglasses, she scanned the rooftop. "You were just arriving, and I was on my way to meet a friend."

The man smiled and took his sunglasses off. "Ah, now I remember. You took my cab."

"I wasn't aware it was yours."

"I'd just come from a meeting," he said, smiling again. His blue eyes seemed to sparkle with mischief. "Just needed to grab my bags from the boat, before catching a flight here."

Is this guy following me? Charity wondered. *Does he know something?*

Taking one of the phony business cards from her purse, she extended it to the man. "Gabby Fleming, I'm a photo-journalist with *Tropical Luxury Magazine*."

Taking the card with his left hand, he reached across Charity's table with his right. "Rene Cook, thrill and adventure junkie."

Charity took his offered hand. "What kind of thrills brought you all the way across the Caribbean without your boat?"

"Mango festival," he replied with a sheepish grin.

The wind had blown a strand of hair across her face; Charity pushed it behind her ear. "Mangos?"

"Best in the world," he replied, studying her card and frowning. "I assume you're here for work, not for plea-sure?"

Satisfied that there wasn't anyone on the roof paying the two of them any attention, Charity decided that Rene was no threat, and smiled. "Is there a rule that a person can't combine the two?"

Rene stood up suddenly. "Excuse me, I just remembered I have an appointment. Nice meeting you."

"Sure," Charity said, somewhat annoyed. "See you around."

As he walked past, Charity noticed the same cologne that she'd smelled in the taxi. She followed him with her eyes as he wove through the tables toward the elevator.

The waiter interrupted her, asking if she were ready to order. When she looked again, Rene was gone. The elevator door opened and several more teenagers got out.

"I've changed my mind," she told the waiter as she stood up, leaving a five-dollar bill on the table. "I'm going to have dinner in my room."

The elevator opened instantly, when she pushed the down button. Nobody was inside. She stepped in and the door closed. The only scent in the small box was coconut suntan oil.

How could the man have disappeared from a rooftop? Charity wondered.

When she reached her room, Charity went to her laptop and powered it up. She typed a quick message, asking if there was another asset in the country besides Thurman Napier. She saved it, then went inside and used the desk phone to call room service.

When she returned to the balcony, there was a new saved message. *No, why do you ask?*

She quickly described meeting Rene, and her suspicions, giving a complete description of the man, then saved it. The reply came just a few seconds later.

> *Your quarry may have contacts in PoS. Proceed with caution.*
> *—TS*

Charity decided that it would probably be best if she limited being seen for as long as she was here. She opened the file on her target and began to read through it again, much more slowly, while she waited for room service.

CHAPTER FIFTEEN:

Rene managed to leave the rooftop, by way of the stairway behind the bar, without anyone noticing. When he reached his room, he went straight to his laptop. He'd recognized the woman instantly when she got off the elevator.

The Caribbean was over a million square miles, with thousands of islands. Cook's instincts told him that the chances of seeing the same person on two islands hundreds of miles apart were very low—almost non-existent. But there was a slim chance that it was just coincidence. While he waited for the laptop to boot up, he examined the business card the woman had given him.

The font and raised texture of the words were all too familiar. He set it aside and dug through his computer bag until he found another business card, which he placed beside the woman's.

Logging onto the hotel's wifi, he searched Google for the woman's name, but found nothing connected to photography. When he searched for the name of the company she worked for, he found quite a few hits. Searching again, with the woman's name and the business name both in quotes, Google came up with only five results. He clicked on the first one and waited.

Cook studied the two business cards, side by side. The words were different, as was the logo, of course. But he'd been trained to look beyond the obvious and he felt pretty certain both cards were from the same source. Maybe not the same exact office, but he felt pretty certain they were both from the American government. He knew the one from his bag was fake, and felt pretty certain the woman's card was, also.

The business card from his computer bag was one of his own. He rarely used them when he worked for Central Intelligence, unless they were phony and he was under-cover. His job description entailed not being known.

The name on the cards he used now, Rene Cook, was an alias—as was the name of his boat. He'd come up with the name himself, taken from a novelist whose books he enjoyed. But the novelist had spelled the first name Renee, the feminine version. His new cards had been printed by a friend, and sent to him through a series of contacts. His passport and other identification had been created by the same friend in Coconut Grove, a suburb of Miami. The business cards he'd printed were different paper, with no raised letters.

The guy lived off the grid, in a way. He was a comput-er hacker and gamer who rarely ventured outside his small house. Everything he needed, he purchased on the Internet and had shipped to his house. His groceries were delivered weekly. No, Marcus wouldn't be the one who divulged where Rene was located. All he knew was that Rene was somewhere in the Caribbean.

A couple who lived aboard their yacht at the marina on Grand Cayman were keeping an eye on his boat while he was away. He didn't like leaving his boat, but he didn't want to miss the annual festival. Weather delays in the Caymans put him beyond the window he could sail here.

Rene checked his email. Nothing from the couple in the next slip. He composed a quick note to them that he'd arrived safely and innocently asked if everything was okay there. He sent the message and sat back in the chair to think, while staring out the glass sliding door at the water. The sun was nearing the horizon.

A few minutes later, his laptop pinged. It was a reply from the couple looking after his boat. From the woman, it seemed, though they shared a single email address. She wrote that Ken was still out on a dive and everything at the marina was boring and she was going to go shopping. No mention of anyone around his boat.

Cook had once been a field agent with the CIA. His specialty was the Caribbean and South America and, for a time, he'd been an attaché at the American embassy in Bogota. He'd left the clandestine service nearly two years ago, fed up with the politics. He knew enough to permanently retire a number of U.S. congressmen and senators, as well as a few high-ranking people in the military.

Disappearing was something Victor Pitt, also known as Rene Cook, Simon Campbell, Will Souther, and several other aliases, was very good at. His code name with the Agency had been Smoke, because he could disappear in a puff of it.

If Gabby Fleming, or whatever her name really was, was an agent on his tail, she was sloppy. He knew the Agency wanted him back—or, at the very least, dead. Would they send a sloppy agent after him?

He decided he needed to be certain if the Agency had picked up his trail. He'd shadow the woman. If she really was after him, she'd tip her hand sooner or later. If so, one or the other of them would disappear in a puff of smoke.

And the nature of the smoke would be his choosing.

CHAPTER SIXTEEN:

Before dawn, Charity was dressed in jeans and a long-sleeved work shirt. She'd eaten breakfast in her room an hour before sunrise. She checked the hall in both directions, before walking quickly from her room to the elevator with her flight bag.

In the lobby, the only person in sight was the clerk at the desk, who smiled as Charity walked past. She nodded to the young man and continued out to the waiting taxi. She saw nobody outside, and looked out the back window of the cab several times during the short ride to the airport.

Minutes later, the driver dropped her off at the private aviation terminal. She looked all around and saw that there wasn't a soul in sight, and the parking lot was empty. The door was locked, but they'd given her a key card like hotels used. She swiped the card; the door buzzed and she pulled it open, then went inside. Though it could be accessed by private aircraft owners, the private terminal wasn't manned twenty-four hours like the main terminal.

Stepping out the back door to the tarmac, she again scanned the area. Hers was the only helicopter, but there were several small private planes and two larger corporate jets. They all sat silently in the dim yellowish glow of the lights around the apron and the sun just about to rise over the mountains.

She walked out to her bird, did a hasty walk-around, and released the tie-downs. Then she unlocked and slid the back door open, quickly climbing inside and closing it behind her. She opened the storage hatch and pushed the release for the false bottom, then lifted it out and removed her Sig from beneath it, sticking the gun into her flight bag.

Climbing into the left seat, Charity stowed the bag under it and strapped in. She went through a quick preflight, raised the wheels to avoid a torque spin, then started the turbine. The sound was unusually loud in the quiet morning air.

Getting clearance from the tower, Charity lifted the chopper a few feet off the ground and, in the gathering light of day, taxied to the runway. In minutes, she was climbing and headed towards a gap in the mountains several miles to the east.

If the man she'd met was following her, Charity felt pretty confident that she'd left unseen by anyone besides the hotel clerk and the taxi driver.

Ahead, the peaks rose up sharply and Charity flew straight toward the highest one, knowing there was a gap just south of it and Napier's land would be just beyond that.

As she banked right through the gap, the sun suddenly appeared. It hung just above crystal blue water to the east, though the west side of the island was still in the shade of the mountains. She put on her sunglasses and pointed the nose downward, following the contours of the mountain slope.

There were a few scattered farms, but Napier's place was pretty easy to find. The strobe on the roof of his hangar set his apart from the farm houses, even in the bright sunlight of the new day.

Noting a tattered windsock at the end of the short airstrip, she turned slightly to approach upwind and gently set the bird down in the grass at the end of the strip.

As the rotors slowed, a large man stepped out of the hangar. He was taller than just about any man Charity had seen outside the freak shows her father had taken her to as a girl. His hair and beard were wild, and he wore a patch over his left eye.

Gee thanks, Colonel, Charity thought. *You don't want me to attract any attention and then you give me a gargantuan pirate for a guide.*

Climbing out of the helo with her flight bag, Charity put it over her right shoulder, her hand inside gripping the Sig as the big man approached her.

"Thurman Napier?"

"Yeah," the man grunted. "And you must be Gabby Fleming. Or is that an alias?"

"Yeah," Charity said, by way of a reply. "Are you ready to go?"

"Not so fast," Napier replied. "I got a few questions, first. And take your hand off that pea-shooter before you hurt someone."

"Mister Napier, I was told you'd be helpful and cooperative."

"I might be a sight more helpful if you don't shoot my ass by accident. As far as cooperation—you need me, I don't need you."

Looking around the dilapidated hangar and at the house beyond it, Charity removed her sunglasses. "Looks to me like you could use any help you can get."

Napier laughed, which brought on a fit of coughing. When he finally got it together, he fixed his one eye on Charity for a moment. "Look, lady. I don't need help from anyone. That private terminal you flew out of? I own it. I also own most of this side of the Aripo range and, if I was so inclined, I could buy and sell you and Colonel Stockwell."

"Somehow I doubt that," Charity said, removing her hand from the flight bag, but leaving it open.

"I introduced toilet paper to people on the river," Napier said. With a grin, he added, "Really cleaned up."

"On toilet paper?"

"Last time I checked, my net worth was about five million."

Charity eyed him closer. Nothing about him spoke of wealth, and there was nothing in his bio to indicate it, though his bio was mostly empty after dropping off the grid in the late seventies.

"So why are you helping?"

Napier jerked a thumb behind him. "Mostly for kicks, but the Colonel said I get to keep the boat."

Charity noticed the boat for the first time. It sat back in the gloom inside the hangar and was painted nearly all black.

"Is that the boat you're going to take me upriver in?"

"If you're fool enough to go, yeah."

Charity walked past the big man, entering the hangar. When she spoke, her words echoed off the metal walls and roof of the hangar. "What're your questions?"

"Not a lot of choppers around here. What's the range?"

Stepping up closer to the boat, she noticed that it was a catamaran. "She has auxiliary fuel cells, which are full. At cruising speed, I can cover the four hundred miles easily."

"And you're qualified to fly backcountry? There ain't no airports or even a wide spot to set down, where we're going."

"I'm qualified," Charity replied, turning back to Napier, who stood in the open door. "And I'm in a hurry. Are you coming with me or not?"

"You got stones," Napier said, with a chuckle. "I'll give you that. Yeah, I'll guide you. And if you still want me to take you upriver, I'll tote your cute ass up there. Odds are I'll never see you again, though. You go into that jungle, you'll end up as croc and piranha shit on the river bottom."

"Let's get in the air, then," Charity said, ignoring both taunts.

Ten minutes later, they were in the air, swooping down toward the east coast, before turning south and flying low over the water, just half a mile offshore. She really felt good, being back in the air.

"Stick to the coastline," Napier said. "It's about sixty miles to the point at Galeota. Then turn right to a heading of two-three-zero and hold that for fifty miles to the delta. Where you wanna go is ninety river miles from the delta. Shorter if you fly a straight line over all the twists and turns."

"We'll show up on radar if we fly high over the jungle."

"What radar?" Napier said. "You gotta get all this tech-no-modern shit outa your mind. You're going back in time a couple thousand years down there."

Charity considered what he'd said. The route he described would be almost exactly half her fuel. "How far is it in a straight line?"

"No clue," he replied. "I was never fool enough to fly anything down there."

"Best guess?" Charity asked looking over at him. He was looking straight ahead through the windshield, so all she saw was his left profile, with the eye patch. Below the patch, mostly covered by his graying beard, she could see a long jagged scar.

"Flying straight from Galeota to the island in the river? Probably cuts thirty miles from the distance."

"Any place to refuel in Galeota?"

"Nope."

"Near the island?"

"Nope," Napier replied again. "I'm tellin' ya, this is beyond Third World. There ain't even electricity for a hundred miles of where you're going. The airport you left is the closest one to where you're going."

Charity flew on in silence for a few minutes, the new port at Galeota coming into sight.

"We'll follow the river going in," she said finally. "Coming back, we make a beeline for the airport at Port of Spain."

"I got about two hundred gallons of kerosene in the hangar and another two hundred gallons of regular gas. Mix 'em right and you have a pretty decent replacement for Jet-A."

Charity looked over to see him grinning at her. "I'll stick with the airport fuel," she said.

CHAPTER
SEVENTEEN:

The sun was slowly burning off the morning fog. The mist hung in the air just above the water, rising up to the high jungle canopy along the shore. Karl Aleksander shoved off from the pier and engaged the boat's transmission. It had been several days since he'd delivered the seed to the old man and his neighbor. The babo wanted to know if they had planted it.

The only other person on the boat was the man they called *Botaniker*. Not that he had any kind of formal education in botany, but Hans Gruber had always preferred plants over people. He'd found a number of plants deep in the jungle that he was unable to identify in his dozens of books.

Lately, Gruber had been working on cross-pollinating different sub-species of the coca plant. There were only four known species, three being cultivated and one that grew wild on the eastern slopes of the Andes. From his research, Gruber had felt certain that there was a fifth ancestral form of the plant and he'd located it, deep in the highland jungle.

"Are you sure you can tell what they planted?" Karl asked.

"You said they planted four days ago. The shoots should be sprouting today."

"That is not what I asked," Karl growled, spinning the wheel to dodge a large crocodile swimming in the shallow water, with what looked like a half-grown tapir in its mouth.

"From the shoots, it is easy to tell if they are coca plants," the *botaniker* said. "In a week, they will be half a meter tall. I developed the plant to grow very fast."

They continued in relative silence for several more minutes, until they reached the southern end of the land their grandfathers had settled more than sixty years earlier.

As they rounded a curve in the river, the wall came into view. Extending twenty feet out into the water from the bank, it was an impressive sight—built four meters in height, with each plank ten centimeters thick and set two meters into the ground. They were locked together with five-centimeter tongue-and-groove joinery and iron hasps, creating a solid wall that would stop a speeding truck. It was more than enough to keep out the jungle animals.

"What were they thinking when they built that?" Hans asked.

"Our forefathers had powerful enemies," Karl replied, as he watched the men and women at work in the fields. The gate keepers were also farmers and hunters. They supplied most of the food for the community, hunting in the jungle and raising crops on the three kilometer by one hundred meter clearing.

From shore to shore, the island had been clear-cut in a straight line, the clearing more than two hundred meters wide. The caracoli trees, which the great wall had been built from, had a natural defense against insects and rot, even buried in the muck at the shoreline. Deadfalls in the jungle took hundreds of years to decay.

Coming alongside the wall, Karl brought the boat down to an idle, matching the flow of the river and holding the boat steady against the current. The island was nearly flat, rising only two meters above the river at its highest point here. From the boat, Karl could almost see the other side of the island three kilometers across the clearing.

There was a door in the wall that allowed access to the other side. A small group of men lived with their families close to the wall, their homes set back into the woods a few meters from the clearing. On the jungle side of the wall, native plants grew like they did everywhere else in the jungle: very fast. It was the job of these men to keep the area on the other side of the wall clear and to maintain the wall itself. Karl had been out to the wall, many times. It didn't need much in the way of maintenance. In fact, in the sixty years of its existence, there hadn't been a single panel that needed to be replaced.

"I still think it looks ugly," the smaller man said, pushing his eyeglasses up on his nose.

"Your thoughts do not matter, *Botaniker*," Karl hissed. "The babo says we need it, so we need it."

Karl finally spotted her thick mane of blond hair, as she carried a basket of vegetables out of the garden toward one of the houses. Jenifer Wirth was more than ten years younger than Karl, still a girl really. She was sixteen years old and the daughter of one of the gate keepers.

Jenifer saw Karl looking, and waved. He waved back as her father came out of the field. Erik Wirth was a giant of a man, bigger than Karl. Wirth didn't like Karl, nor did he like his daughter associating with him.

Karl gunned the engine and the boat sped away. *Wirth will just have to get used to the idea*, Karl thought. He'd chosen Jenifer years earlier, and made it known to the other single men in the community. The council had approved the union, even over the father's protests.

Marriages in the small community had to be closely monitored and both parties' pedigrees examined carefully. This had been instituted long before Karl was born, to prevent inbreeding as much as possible. Girls were made available to prospective husbands on their fourteenth birthdays and married at seventeen. Karl had made it clear a week before Jenifer's fourteenth birthday that he would kill anyone who applied to be her suitor. He and Jenifer were scheduled to be united in just a few months.

A few minutes later, Karl slowed the boat as they neared Vicente Navarro's land. Turning the boat, Karl idled toward shore. Just as the keel made contact with the bottom, he gunned the engine for a moment, driving the boat up onto shore. He quickly shut down the engine and went forward, vaulting over the bow and pulling the boat further up onto shore. The water level rose only when the floods came, so he usually didn't bother to tie the boat off to anything.

"Let us go see what they are growing," Karl said to Gruber.

At the top of the low riverbank, Karl easily saw that most of the cassava plants were gone. Only a few rows remained near the old man's hut. Where the cassava had once stood were now hundreds of rows of furrowed dirt. Tiny green plants only a couple of centimeters tall and a meter apart sprouted up in straight lines, thousands of them.

Gruber trudged past Karl, heading straight for the nearest row. There, he knelt by the tiny plants. "These are definitely my coca plants," he muttered, looking down the length of the row. A short man with long white hair was approaching.

Hans stood up, as Karl came up beside him. "Is that the farmer?"

"Yes, his name is Vicente Navarro," Karl answered. "He is supposed to be some kind of shaman or something."

The two watched as the old man came nearer. When he was close enough, Karl pointed to where the old crops still grew. "Why do you still grow cassava?"

The shaman didn't answer until he was just a few meters away, where he stopped and looked at the two white men. "The cassava near the jungle grows slower. They will ripen soon."

"You were told to harvest it all and plant the coca."

Vicente turned and looked back at the few remaining rows, still shaded from the late morning sun by the jungle just beyond his house. When he turned back, he shrugged. "Planting the coca there will do no good. It will never mature before the floods come."

Karl started to say something, but Hans interrupted. "He is right. The coca will grow tall very fast, but the alkaloid content will be poor, at best. The plants need full sunlight."

Vicente nodded slightly to Hans. "We can plant there if you wish. But it will lower the price of the crop as a whole."

"How can a few poor quality plants bring down the price of the others?" Karl asked, unconvinced.

"He is right again," Hans said, returning the old man's nod. "The leaves will look just like those from the plants in the sun, but they will be far less potent. The chemicals used for extraction would be wasted on those leaves."

"Fine," Karl sneered. "Keep the cassava."

In the distance, all three men heard a beating sound, as if someone were hammering quickly on a large bass drum. The sound rose in intensity, then faded for a moment. It rose, this time louder, and faded again.

"What is that?" Hans asked, staring toward the tree line at the north end of Vicente's property. "Thunder?"

The sound grew steadily louder, rising and falling in intensity. Karl shielded his eyes against the glare of the sun, scanning the treetops for the source of the noise. Suddenly, a large black machine came over the trees, following the river. Karl had seen small airplanes fly over before and knew what they were. He'd seen pictures of this sort of machine, but had never personally seen a helicopter before.

Flying past where Karl had beached the boat, the helicopter climbed quickly. At the apex of the climb, it swooped around in a tight turn, then came back down to treetop level. The front of the thing was pointed toward them as it came to a stop over the river. The whirring blades caused spray to come off the water beneath them and created thousands of round ringlet waves, like so many stones being tossed into the still water. The trees that lined the riverbank bent and swayed, then the force of the wind hit the men in the field like a gale, kicking up dust from the dry ground.

Karl ran quickly for the boat, where he'd left his rifle. Jumping over the gunwale, he pulled the rifle from its rack next to the helm and brought it up to his shoulder. The wind-generated waves from the helicopter rocked the boat as he aimed and fired.

The helicopter rolled violently sideways, then dropped its nose and accelerated downriver, just a meter above the deadly water. In seconds, it had disappeared beyond the trees. Karl followed the sound and saw the helicopter again as it rose above the jungle canopy, its nose low, accelerating away to the north.

CHAPTER EIGHTEEN:

Though he was strapped in tightly, Thurman gripped the grab rail with one hand and his seat with the other. Charity followed the river, only a few feet above the water, whipping around each cutback in the river, turning the chopper nearly on its side at times.

Any doubt he'd had about her ability in the back country vanished in the first fifteen miles of river flying. Glancing over at her, he thought she looked as if she were out for a drive in the country. With her right hand on the stick in front of her and her left hand down at her side on the other control, she seemed to move with the chopper as if they were one.

"I take back anything I said about your flying ability, lady," Thurman said into the little boom mic in front of his mouth.

Charity glanced at the giant in the passenger seat. Even with the secondary controls removed, he filled the whole right side of the aircraft. It appeared as if at any moment he was going to pull the grab rail off the side of the windshield frame.

"Relax, Mister Napier. Grab your shoulder harness. It's easier to control your upper body than those grab bars."

Thurman looked over at her again. She was totally relaxed and actually seemed to be enjoying herself. He released his death grip on the rail and seat, and grabbed his shoulder restraints.

"You're gonna have to follow the river on the return. I'm pretty sure my stomach is just a couple miles back."

Charity glanced over and smiled. "You're holding on wrong," she said. "Cross your arms."

Doing as he was told, Thurman did feel more secure and in control of his body. They'd dropped down below the treetops a mile upriver from the delta, and he was pretty sure he had bruises on his legs and right shoulder from being banged around.

"Better slow down," Thurman said. "The northern tip of the island is coming up in another mile or so."

Charity put the bird into a slow climb, bleeding off speed as she rose higher for a better view. At two hundred feet, she could see over the jungle canopy. Her eyes saw nothing but green all the way to the far horizon. The tops of the trees seemed to be mostly all the same height. Here and there, mist clung to low spots, the horizon hazy but brilliant blue above.

"It looks just like you said," Charity commented in awe. "Like some other world."

"Out here," Thurman began, "things just ain't really all that far removed from the primordial ooze our distant ancestors crawled out of."

Charity continued to follow the river, just above the trees. Part of the landscape ahead was different. The jungle didn't look as thick, and there was a haze hanging over it.

Thurman saw her notice it and said, "That's the brotherhood's settlement. Can you imagine what life was like when they first came here?"

"Brotherhood?"

"Stockwell didn't tell you?"

"Tell me what?" Charity asked.

They rounded another bend in the river and a dock came into view. After ninety miles of flying, seeing only two loincloth-clad men paddling canoes, the dock seemed incongruent to its surroundings, an insult to the tranquility Charity had felt in the place as she wove the chopper upstream. The river seemed to split on either side of the dock, both branches equal in size.

Beyond the dock, homes and buildings could be seen, set back among a stand of trees. To Charity's eyes, it appeared as if the jungle had been thinned and all the undergrowth removed. A little town had been built among the trees.

The architecture and layout of the buildings she could see looked like a throwback to the middle of the last century. If there had been rolling hills, she'd have guessed she was somewhere in Southern Europe.

"The man you're after? The babo? He's the leader of the brotherhood," Thurman said, as Charity slowed the chopper to a crawl, looking down at the community. "The brotherhood are the descendants of German soldiers, Nazis, who escaped and came here after Dubya Dubya Two."

"Nazis?" Charity asked.

Thurman looked over at her as she turned the chopper, following the eastern branch of the river. "Yeah, they came here in 1945, so I'm told. Bought the north end of this island that separates the two branches of the Manamo, and built a settlement here."

"War criminals?"

"Maybe. Who knows? The people living down there are their descendants. The founders are all long dead."

"How do they survive all the way out here in the jungle?"

The big man shrugged. "They fish and hunt, I guess. Just like the Indians. They have a farm on the north end of their property and a huge wall that keeps the jungle out."

A few people could be seen far below, coming out of homes and stores to look up at the helicopter.

"As much as I prefer this dawdling speed," Thurman said. "it's probably best if we move along. The brotherhood don't take kindly to intruders."

Checking the fuel gauge, Charity said, "We still have thirty minutes of play time. I want to see this wall—and anything else upriver—until we're bingo fuel."

Charity put the bird into a shallow dive, gaining speed and moving upriver. Away from the main part of the settlement, through the treetops, she could see more homes and other buildings, scattered across the huge island. She estimated there were at least a hundred structures.

"How many people live there?" she asked.

"Nobody but the brotherhood knows for sure. I'd guess near a thousand. It's said there were only about twenty when they first got here. Mostly men."

Charity turned and looked at Napier. "From fewer than ten women in 1945, there are now a thousand descendants? That's only three or four generations."

"Five," Thurman corrected. "Maybe six. They have planned marriages, men select their wives when they're fourteen and can marry them at seventeen."

Charity considered that. Even with large families, there shouldn't be that many people in an isolated community only five or six generations later. "You seem to know quite a bit about these people."

"They've taken in others from time to time," he said. "To keep the gene pool fresh and grow larger. I joined up with them in seventy-three."

Charity glanced at him.

He rubbed the empty socket under the eyepatch and said, "We sort of had a falling out."

"Is that how you lost your eye?" she asked, point blank.

Thurman looked over, meeting her steady gaze with his one eye. "It's how my face got cut open. Lost the eye to infection."

Charity didn't need Thurman to tell her where the southern edge of the settlement was. The jungle had been clear-cut from shore to shore in a hideous straight line that looked like it ran straight east to west.

Like a single board turned on its edge, a giant wall ran down the center of the cleared area. It looked old but sturdy, rising at least ten or twelve feet high.

The wall was unbroken for its whole length, the ends set several yards out into the river. Crops extended out from the wall to the tree line on one side. The brighter green of the cultivated area contrasted sharply with the dark green of the jungle.

Charity could see people working in the field. Men, women, and children all looked up as the chopper flew by just a hundred feet above the water.

On the other side of the wall, an area equal in size to the farm was mostly grass or bare dirt. Nothing grew more than a couple of feet tall on that side. Looking back through the side window, Charity could see that there was a heavy door set in the middle of the wall. She guessed it was to allow workers access to the jungle side to make repairs. Slipping into the settlement from that side would be suicide if they had sentries.

"How difficult would it be to get onto the island underwater at night?" Charity asked, thinking it would be best to use a rebreather and go ashore under cover of darkness.

"Ha," Thurman barked. "Difficult don't even begin to get into the discussion. Crocs and caimans hunt at night. Then there's piranha. Black piranha, the biggest species there is." He pointed down through the windshield. "They're as thick in that water as stars in the night sky. The locals call them caribes. There's a cannibal tribe named after them. Mostly gone now, except for a small population on Dominica, up in the Windwards."

Charity dropped the helo lower, following the river at a slightly slower speed, looking for a place where a boat could land. She wasn't at all concerned that the slow fly-by might tip off her adversary. Ready or not, she'd find a way to get close enough to kill the man she'd been sent to kill.

The jungle looked impenetrable. The trees at the edge of the water had a tangle of roots and deadfalls that appeared to go deep into the jungle. Spotting a huge fallen tree on the outside of a sharp turn in the river, Charity slowed as she approached

"What do you make of that dead tree in the water?" she asked.

"As a means of entry? It could work. The base is above the roots and the water will be plenty deep on the outside of the curve. Looks fresh, might not be too slippery."

"What's further south?" Charity asked.

"Farms a few miles ahead, on the south end of the island. Just past there is a little village called Tucupita. Most of the younger men of the village work on the farms."

As Charity turned the chopper around another tight bend in the river, the land to the west opened up into cultivated farmland, stretching the width of the island all the way to the southern tip. She made out a number of lines separating one parcel from another, wooden fences and tall reeds. Each parcel had one or two small huts, usually set in the middle of the farm.

Suddenly, a boat appeared around a curve in the river. Unlike the few wooden canoes they'd seen, this was a sleek-looking powerboat, pulled up onto the riverbank.

"Hang on!" Charity exclaimed, as she pulled back on the cyclic. The nose of the chopper came up and they climbed steeply, the rotors beating hard against the air.

As the chopper slowed, she pushed the right pedal to the floor, kicking the heavy helicopter around as she pushed the cyclic forward.

"Mother Mary!" Thurman shouted, as the river seemed to rush up to meet them.

Charity pulled up on the collective, bringing the Huey to a stop just twenty feet above the river. The nose pointed toward three men standing on shore at the edge of a newly furrowed field.

Two of the men were white, the third obviously an indigenous Indian. The Indian's hair was long and gray and Charity thought, even from fifty yards away, that he looked vaguely familiar.

One of the men suddenly darted away from the other two. He was a big man, wearing jeans, a long-sleeved work shirt, and a wide-brimmed hat.

"I know that guy!" Thurman said. "He's sort of the head of security for the brotherhood. Name's Karl Aleksander." They watched as the man boarded the boat and moved to the helm.

"Gun!" Thurman shouted, needlessly.

Charity's hand on the stick was already moving, yanking the chopper violently to the right. At the same time, her subconscious registered the fact that the rifle had recoiled against the shooter's shoulder. She didn't hear a bullet smacking through the thin aluminum skin, nor did she feel it, so she assumed for now that he'd missed. She made a mental note in her conscious mind to check the bird thoroughly when she got back. Another part of her mind, the part she usually kept a tight lid on, opened and closed for just a moment, recording the man's face in every detail.

She pushed the stick forward, dipping the nose precariously toward the water, as she hauled up on the collective, nearly red-lining the torque. The bird responded quickly to her deft movements on the controls, flying nose down, increasing speed back the way they'd come.

Approaching the bend in the river that they'd just come around, Charity pulled back on the stick and the chopper leapt upward, pushing them both down into their seats. She lowered the collective, bringing her bird back to level flight only twenty feet above the treetops.

"Hot damn!" Thurman exclaimed exuberantly. "You fly this thing like it's part of you."

"That guy shot at us!" Charity exclaimed. "What the hell for?"

"Because we were there," Thurman replied. "Aleksander's a fucking nut-job. He keeps a tight fist on everyone down here. If you're an outsider, you have the life expectancy of a mosquito."

"Who was the old Indian man?"

"Local farmer, by the name of Vicente Navarro. He's a medicine man of the boat people."

"Boat people?"

"The Ye'kuana. They've lived here since the dawn of time."

"For all that rifleman knew, we could have been the law!"

Thurman looked at Charity as she glanced over. He didn't see fear on her face, but even through her dark sunglasses, he could see a burning fury in her eyes. His voice was foreboding when he spoke. "There ain't no law down here, except what a man carries in with him."

CHAPTER NINETEEN:

Watching as the two men left in their boat, Vicente called out to the two young boys, hiding in the field. He'd told them to lie down between the furrows when the boat arrived with the white men. As one, the young field workers rose and trotted quickly to the side of the shaman.

"What was that, Buyei?" the older of the two boys asked. "I have never seen such a thing."

"It made its own wind," the second boy said, brushing the dust from his hair.

The old man smiled. "Yes, it made its own wind. Take your *bongos* and spread word to the elders. Tell them to come here when *Choco* rises above the trees. Tell them to come to the ceremonial place and be prepared for a welcome ritual."

The two boys looked at each other, puzzled. Then they turned and sprinted across the field to the spot where they'd pulled their canoes out of the water and hidden them under the brush. Since the shaman's boat had been destroyed, Vicente had told them to keep their boats out of sight while working.

Vicente wasn't just a farmer, nor was he just a shaman, or a canoe maker. He hadn't been much older than his two field workers when he'd left the jungle and returned years later as a middle-aged man. Between those times, Vicente had seen the outside world. He'd worked aboard the great ships that carried products all around the world outside the jungle. He'd seen how small his jungle home was in the vastness of the real world. He'd ridden in automobiles and trains, flown in airplanes, visited faraway lands—and he knew what a helicopter was.

Vicente's entry into the world outside the jungle had come during a time of world-wide growth and prosperity. As a boy, he hadn't been aware of the war waging all across the globe. He remembered the first time he saw a white man. He remembered the time when a group of them took over the downriver side of the island his people lived on.

He remembered when he'd first become aware of the march of time outside his jungle home. In the jungle, time was measured by the passing of the sun and moon, and by the regular floods of the river. The captain of the boat he crewed had shown him a calendar and explained how time had been recorded and could be predicted. The captain had told him about his god and how all time was measured before and after that god's mortal life. He'd told Vicente that his god had walked among his people almost two thousand years ago. He taught Vicente that a year was the time from one flood to the next.

Vicente remembered how, when he was a boy, his father would prepare for the coming flood, knowing almost to the day when it would occur. Gathering seed before the flood was important. When the flood waters receded, it would be time to plant again.

He recalled how the river rose above its bank, forcing people into their homes and compelling them to move about in *bongos* instead of walking on the ground. The captain had told him that it was the year 1950, and guessed that Vicente had been born in the year 1935.

All this had been many years ago. Vicente was an old man now. The babies he'd seen born when he returned to his people were now the tribal elders. The *nibora* who helped him in the fields were the grandchildren of those babies. Because of his time outside the jungle, and the encroachment of that outside world, he knew that the current year was 2007 and he knew that he was seventy-eight years old. He didn't want to know these things, and didn't like them.

His return to his ancestral roots was literally a lifetime ago, but Vicente remembered the things he'd seen. He remembered the things he'd seen others do. He'd wasted his best years doing what he thought would bring prosperity to his family and his people.

All these memories came to the front of his mind, when the helicopter had arrived. He knew what it was. The *nibora* had been right; it did make its own wind. And it rode on that wind.

He'd seen with his own eyes how men flew these machines, how they made them lift off the ground, gracefully rising into the sky and then flying slowly away. The person in control of this black helicopter hadn't done that. The person controlling this machine had made it do things Vicente had never seen.

Minutes later, the two *nibora* passed where Vicente stood on the bank of the river, both of them paddling hard against the slight current near shore. Vicente waited until they were completely out of sight, then turned and stared toward where the black machine had risen above the jungle and disappeared. He gazed northward for several minutes, listening. The roar of the machine had long since vanished on the wind.

Finally, Vicente walked slowly toward his house. Part of him felt like kicking the small plants that had just that morning sprung up from the ground. In his soul, he knew these plants would never be used for the white men's drug.

The farmer in him took mercy on the tiny, defenseless plants. Besides, he knew the coca leaves had other uses besides the making of cocaine, beneficial uses. When the *itoto* were gone, he and the other farmers could share the crop among the people to make tea. The shaman knew the leaves could be chewed to ease pain and suffering.

When Vicente reached his home, he picked up his bag and flung the strap across one shoulder, continuing past the house to the jungle. He'd left a third of his land as it was, when he cleared the rest for farming. This seemed as though it was only days ago, but had been when his hair was still mostly black.

Following a narrow path into the dense jungle, he soon found himself in a small clearing. He went about preparing for the ritual. In minutes, he'd gathered several clumps of dried moss and added a few twigs. Using a small bow from his pouch, he soon had a smoldering fire going, which he blew into.

Gathering more wood, he sat beside the fire, allowing the smoke to pass over him on the light breeze filtering through the trees. Pulling his pouch closer, he took out his pipe and yopo seed. He would try to speak to the warrior spirit, before the elders arrived, to see what it was she wanted them to do.

Choco would rise above the trees not long after the sun fell below them on the other side of the land. The elders would be arriving soon.

The sounds of the jungle around Vicente quieted, telling the old shaman that the elders were arriving, long before they started up the path from his house. He rose from where he'd been sitting for several hours and walked toward the path to greet them.

"Your worker told me what he saw," Guyan Montenegro said, as he approached his old friend. "A black machine that flies like the dragonfly."

Vicente turned and lead Guyan and the others to the fire, taking the place of honor with *Choco's* light in his face. "Yes, that is what we saw, Guyan."

The others arranged themselves in a circle around the small fire, as Vicente loaded his pipe. Before lighting it, he said, "The black machine is controlled by the warrior spirit."

Several men spoke at once, until Guyan raised a hand to quiet them. "The *buyei* wishes us to smoke first."

Vicente already had a twig to the pipe, ignoring the outburst of questions. Drawing a deep breath, he ritually washed the smoke from the pipe's bowl over his head, before passing it to the next man.

Once it had been passed around, Guyan handed the pipe back to Vicente, saying, "We did not expect this for some time yet."

"She never told me when," Vicente replied. "Only that she would arrive."

"How can you know this flying machine is the warrior spirit?" one of the other elders asked.

"Just before you arrived," Vicente began, "I had another visitor. I'd been trying since the machine arrived, but was unable to see until after *Choco* had risen. I was visited by not just the warrior spirit, but the forest mother, as well. The vision was much clearer this time."

"What did they tell you?" Guyan asked.

"The warrior spirit said she needs our help to get to the *itoto* settlement without being seen."

Another of the younger men in the council spoke up. "How can we be sure the spirit who visited you and this black machine are the same?"

"They are not the same," Vicente said. "The spirit uses the black machine as we do our *bongos*."

"The dancer of the wind controls this machine?" Guyan asked.

Slowly, a wry grin spread across the old man's lined face. "It *danced*; on its *own* wind it danced."

CHAPTER TWENTY:

Rene Cook had a good deal of patience. He'd awakened early and had gone down to the parking lot of the hotel, where he kept his rental scooter. His wait hadn't been very long. Half an hour before sunrise, a cab pulled to a stop in front of the hotel. Minutes later, Gabriella Fleming came out and got in the backseat of the taxi and it drove away.

With the scooter's lights turned off, he'd followed at a distance. The woman had come to the airport where he now continued to wait. Minutes after her arrival, a black helicopter with the name *Tropical Luxury Magazine* stenciled on the side doors had flown off toward the mountains.

It was now nearly noon and she hadn't returned. *Maybe she really is what she says*, Rene thought. But his gut instinct told him otherwise.

So he continued waiting patiently. He'd left the scooter on the upwind end of the airstrip. It was only a few feet off the road, but completely swallowed up by the jungle undergrowth, and invisible to passersby.

Near the airport fence, he'd climbed a tree and now sat comfortably on a large branch, with his back against the trunk. His pack hung on the stump of a smaller branch, just beside him. In the pack was enough food, in the form of meals-ready-to-eat, to last him all day and all night, if need be.

As a field agent with the CIA, he'd spent hours, sometimes days, watching from a distance. He'd grown used to the MRE pouches, unlike many other agents who constantly complained about the bland taste.

Another hour passed, the seventh since he'd climbed up in the tree. In the distance, he began to hear the faint beating sound of a helicopter. It echoed slightly as it came through the high pass to the east, most of the sound absorbed by the thick jungle. Moments later, he spotted the black chopper and trained his field glasses on it, as it flew west on the north side of the airport.

Minutes later, he could see it again, as the helo descended toward the airstrip directly in front of him. As it got nearer, the powerful binoculars brought the cockpit into sharp focus. Gabriella Fleming appeared to be alone, focused on her approach behind a pair of dark aviator-type sunglasses.

Once the chopper was finally on the ground, Rene continued to watch as she climbed out and walked all the way around the bird, inspecting every square inch of the fuselage.

Finally, she turned toward an approaching fuel truck. When it stopped, she climbed up on the running board to talk to the driver, then walked toward the private aviation terminal.

Rene quickly stowed the field glasses in his pack and climbed down from the tree. Riding the scooter, he made it to the parking lot entrance and stopped just as the woman came out and got into a waiting taxi. Rene noticed it was the same cab that had delivered her to the airport this morning.

Again, he followed the taxi at a safe distance all the way back to the hotel. There, the woman paid the cab driver and disappeared through the door to the lobby. He waited five minutes before parking the scooter and going inside himself.

The woman was nowhere to be seen. Approaching the desk, he smiled at the young woman on duty. "Did I just see Gabriella Fleming returning? I was hoping to catch her in the restaurant at dinner time."

The young lady returned his smile. "Yes, sir. She stopped here long enough to order a sandwich to be brought up to her room." She gave him an apologetic look. "Sorry."

"Ah, I guess I'll have to wait and talk to her later, thanks."

Rene took the elevator up to his room and went immediately to his laptop. He wasn't completely devoid of computer skills and had already hacked into the airport's system, so he could keep an eye on arrivals and departures. After a few minutes, he was able to access the fixed base operator's fuel logs. The most recent entry was an FBO sale of three hundred and fifty gallons of Jet-A to *Tropical Luxury Magazine.*

"Interesting," Rene mumbled. *A Huey only has slightly more than a two-hundred-gallon gas tank*, he thought. *She must have an extra tank.*

With a burn rate of seventy or so gallons an hour and a cruising speed of a hundred miles per hour, he quickly calculated that wherever she went it was about four or five hundred miles, round trip.

"That's a lot of ocean," he said to himself. *Going up and over the mountains, probably meant she flew somewhere east of here, but the nearest land going east is Africa. She went over the mountains to pick someone up, then they went either north to the Windwards or south to the mainland.*

"That, or she is what she says she is," he concluded.

CHAPTER TWENTY-ONE:

Charity woke suddenly. She'd been exhausted after dropping Napier at his house and getting the bird back to the airport. She'd checked it over very closely and found no bullet holes, which was good. If someone else noticed one, it would become very suspicious that she'd not reported it. After arranging for fuel, she'd come straight back to the hotel, ordered a sandwich brought up from room service, then eaten and gone to bed.

Looking at the clock on the nightstand, Charity saw that it was just after midnight. She'd been awakened by another dream. This one wasn't like the others that sometimes crept into her sub-conscious at night, though.

Wearing only a faded yellow *Gaspar's Revenge* tee-shirt, Charity stepped out onto the south facing balcony. The shirt was a gift from one of her former co-workers, when she'd spent several weeks on his boat, looking for a man. The friend operated a charter fishing service in the

Florida Keys as a cover. They'd finally tracked the man down and she'd killed him.

The return to the Keys on Jesse McDermitt's boat had been unhurried. Over a period of several days, she'd opened up to the man, more so than with any of the VA shrinks she'd talked with. He had a very easy-going way about him, and she'd felt comfortable when she was around him.

In a moment of loneliness, she wondered where Jesse and her other former co-workers were and what they were doing. It had now been several months since she pulled off of the search for Jesse and flown to Miami to disappear. At times, usually at night, she wondered if they knew what had really happened to her. In ways she couldn't explain or comprehend, it was important to her that the members of her former team, especially McDermitt, know that she wasn't a turncoat, that she hadn't abandoned them.

A crescent moon, halfway up the eastern sky, illuminated the sea and everything on it. Several sailboats lay at anchor in the small bay beneath her. To the southwest, away from the light of the moon and the city, stars flickered against the black background of space.

The dream that had awakened her was puzzling. Most dreams were puzzling, but even more so when you tried to recall them and determine their meaning. In her dream, she'd been talking to the same man that she'd seen in dreams a few times this past week. Those other times, he'd only appeared in a sort of haze, and she was never able to make out any features.

This time, the man was with someone else. A woman. The dream was clearer this time and Charity could tell that both the man and woman were very old. She couldn't recall the woman's features but felt as though she was much older than the man. However, when the woman moved, she carried herself like a much younger woman.

As she stared out over the calm sea, Charity tried to recall the old man's features. She immediately saw the Indian farmer in her mind's eye, standing calmly and looking at the helicopter as if he'd been expecting it. Charity knew it was the farmer she'd seen in previous dreams.

She'd never believed much in the occult, nor was she overly religious. Charity Styles believed in the things she could see, touch, hear, taste, and smell. Outside of those five senses, she just wasn't sure about anything. But Napier had said the man was a witch doctor of some kind.

In the dream, the three of them had talked at length about something very important, but she couldn't recall a single word of the conversation. The old man struck her as a very kind and gentle person, but fiercely loyal—to whom or what, she had no idea. But he seemed to be quite entranced to be in the presence of the old woman.

A slight breeze flattened the tee-shirt against her body, pulling at the hem just below her hips. She stared up at the moon, her hands on the rail, as the gentle breeze caressed her. She closed her eyes and imagined being up there with the moon, looking down on what was taking place below.

Knowing that she wouldn't be able to go back to sleep just yet, Charity went inside and turned on her laptop. She knew that if she posted a message, it would be received immediately and answered as quickly as the information could be attained.

Charity quickly composed an email, giving the names of the old farmer and the head of security, and asking for any intelligence on either of them and more background on Thurman Napier after his separation from the military. When she finished, she read the message, then stepped back out onto the balcony again without saving it.

The wind was blowing a little stronger now, lifting the bottom of the lightweight tee-shirt, exposing her bare body. The only light in the room was the glow from the screen of the laptop and she was six stories up. There was no chance that anyone could see her, so she didn't bother to hold the shirt in place.

She stared up at the moon and again imagined herself being up there. When she closed her eyes, she imagined the parts of the Manamo River she'd seen the day before. Charity imagined looking down on the vast, dark river delta and the surrounding jungle and farmland.

In a startling moment of clarity, with her eyes closed, Charity saw a small campfire near the river, people huddled around it, chanting. Sparks from the fire drifted up toward her along with two words—*move slowly.*

Charity quickly went back inside and added another note to the email before saving it in the drafts folder.

I'll need to borrow Jesse's suit.

CHAPTER TWENTY-TWO:

Sitting at a table in the rooftop restaurant, Rene had a commanding view of the front of the hotel and the road approaching it. If the woman left, it would probably be to go to the airport again. In the hour since dawn, a couple of taxis had arrived and departed, while he sat there drinking coffee. But not the one Gabriella had taken yesterday.

While it might have only been a coincidence that she took the same cab twice, Rene Cook didn't believe in coincidences—and the fact that she did take the same taxi only reinforced his idea that she was with the American government.

The bell-tone rang and he glanced over to see the elevator open. Gabriella Fleming stepped off, with two younger men who appeared to be hitting on her hard enough to leave dents.

She looked around the restaurant, saw him and waved. Then she said something to the two young men and, without waiting for a reply, approached his table.

"Would you mind some company, Mister Cook?" she asked.

"Looks like you were under attack there," Rene replied, wary. He stood and pulled a chair out for her. "Please call me Rene."

"An attack on two fronts," she said, smiling and sitting in the offered chair. "Thank you, Rene."

He sat back down and studied the woman's face. She was strikingly beautiful, with strong features, full lips, and an athletic body. There was something about her that he just couldn't put his finger on. Something just a little off.

Her hair, Rene thought. *Thick and beautiful, but the color or shade doesn't quite fit. She wouldn't be the first woman who dyed her hair at the appearance of the first gray.*

He remained silent, waiting for her to open the conversation.

"You're up early," she finally said.

"I'm always up before the dawn," he replied.

"Why is that?"

The question was innocent enough. Just small talk.

"Not sure, really," Rene replied. "I've just always been one to start the day early. What about you?"

The waiter arrived with a coffee pot and another cup on a small saucer. Gabriella nodded at him and he placed the cup in front of her and filled it. The waiter glanced at Rene, and he nodded as well.

They each took a sip of coffee as the waiter retreated. "I grew up on a farm," she replied. "We always had an hour or two of chores to do before sunrise and breakfast."

He noted her slight accent. "You grew up in Cuba?"

She smiled brightly. "Yes, but we left there when I was just a girl. Escaped during the Mariel boat lift to Florida."

"Ah, I see. But you left at an old enough age that you still have a slight accent."

"I'll save you the math, Rene," Gabriella said with a confident smile. "I'm thirty-three years old."

Rene had in fact been calculating what her age might be, but not for the reason she might have thought.

No more dancing around the subject.

"You sure could have fooled me," he said, smiling back. "Most field agents are younger."

For the briefest moment, her eyes flashed, then returned to the sparkling green they were before. "Field agent?"

"And not a very good one."

Again, her eyes flashed. In that microsecond, Rene sensed that there was something behind them. Something bordering on insane rage or a deep hurt. But he was now certain about who she was.

"Your choice is simple," Rene said flatly. "Report back to your superiors that I disappeared, or you will."

A puzzled look came over her features and, for a moment, Rene thought he might be wrong. Then her hand moved almost imperceptibly toward her bag. When Rene thumbed the hammer on his gun, hidden under the table, she heard it and froze, fear replacing bewilderment in her eyes. The fact that she recognized the sound rein-forced in his mind that his first instinct was correct.

She remained motionless, and an inner confidence again returned to her features. Her voice lowered and the accent disappeared. "I have no idea who or what you are. You are not why I'm here."

"I wish I could believe that, Miss Fleming, or whatev-er your name is."

Her eyes never left his, but she seemed to resign herself to the situation. "My real name's Charity Styles."

"*Agent* Charity Styles," Rene corrected her. "With Central Intelligence?"

"No. Homeland Security."

"Homeland Security? I guess I must have hit the big time."

"I have no idea what you're talking about," she said, a bit of impatience in her voice.

"I know the Agency wants me dead. What'd I do to get DHS onto me?"

Slowly, the woman's expression changed. Not the red-hot rage that had flashed momentarily in her eyes before, but a growing annoyance. "We're three feet apart," she said, in a low and menacing tone. "You will get only one shot, and I won't have to move much to make it a flesh wound. Even injured, I can still kill you before you can pull the trigger a second time."

"You're that confident against an unknown armed adversary?"

"I'm that confident against *any* adversary," she replied.

Looking into this woman's eyes, Rene no longer felt quite as confident. "Why are you here, then?"

"I'm not at liberty to discuss that with anyone," she replied. "But it has nothing to do with you."

"It seems we're at an impasse then," Rene said.

"Yes, it does," she replied. "The way I see it, we can do this one of two ways."

"And those are?"

The rage in her emerald eyes seemed to smolder with a deep burning fire, as if another person were looking at him. "You can pull that trigger, I'll bleed, and you'll die. The second option is you put the gun back in your pocket and we agree to walk away."

Rene had always prided himself on being able to read people. Everyone had a tell, and he was good at picking up on them. Right now, he sensed that she could very well carry out the threat. Most people, when faced with an armed assailant, didn't react this way.

"I'm not after you," she said.

Rene sensed that her body was inwardly coiling like a snake ready to strike, every muscle tensing.

"I don't want to hurt you," she said in a near-whisper. Suddenly Rene felt more vulnerable than he had in his whole life. "But, make no mistake about this: you'll be dead before you can fire a second shot. Make your choice now, Rene. I have things to do."

His instincts had been correct, but he realized he'd mistaken her disinterest in him as poor field craft. She wasn't after him at all, and he fully believed that he was now facing one of the most dangerous people he ever had.

Slowly, Rene decocked the gun and deliberately put it back in his pocket. With a nervous grin, he said, "I believe you."

Without a word, Charity slowly stood up, then turned and walked toward the elevator. One of the two young men who had ridden up with her on the elevator got up from his table and started toward her, his friend just a few steps behind.

Rene remained seated as he watched the man, probably in his early twenties, slim and capable-looking, reach a hand out to grab the woman's shoulder. As soon as his hand touched her, she moved in a blur, spinning into and under his grasp, taking his hand with her, until she pushed it to the back of his neck, nearly lifting the much larger man off his feet.

Both men were caught unaware as Charity yanked up hard on the first man's arm and he screamed in pain. She pushed him away, planted her right foot in the middle of his back, and shoved him into his friend with such force that they both went tumbling to the ground.

"I told you I wasn't interested!" she screamed maniacally at the two men, lying on the floor. Then she disappeared into the elevator.

At his table, a slow, nervous grin crept over Rene's face.

CHAPTER TWENTY-THREE:

Riding down in the elevator, Charity thought about Rene Cook. *Someone who the CIA wants dead?* He seemed to know the inner workings of the nation's top intelligence community. She didn't know a whole lot about the Agency herself, but she knew someone who did.

As soon as she entered her room, she pulled her phone from her purse and made a call. Her standing orders were to never use the phone, except in an emergency. Having a gun unexpectedly pointed at her by someone she didn't know, and had been told was not a threat, seemed like an emergency.

The phone rang five times before Travis Stockwell answered, without preamble. "Is there a problem?"

"The man I spoke of earlier, Rene Cook? He just pointed a gun at me and threatened me."

"Christ," Stockwell muttered. "Tell me where the body is, and I'll move assets to the area to clean things up. This is unfortunate. Will you be able to continue?"

"He's still alive," Charity said. "He seemed to think I was with the CIA and was here after him."

"We came up with nothing on that name, and his passport seemed to be in order. All we found was that he's a former boat builder, now making his way by doing boat repairs."

"It's an alias," Charity said. "He's someone of importance to the Agency."

"Send me a sketch and I'll see what I can come up with. Do you think he's a threat to your mission?"

Charity thought about that for a moment. "No, I don't think he's a threat. But, he definitely thinks the American government wants him dead."

"Get me the sketch. The suit you asked for is on its way. Check with the hotel concierge tomorrow morning for a package."

There was a click, and when Charity looked at the screen she saw that Stockwell had ended the call. She placed the phone on the desk and tore out a sheet from the hotel stationary. Flipping it over, she began to draw from memory.

Twenty minutes later, she had a very good likeness of the man. The hotel's computer probably had a scanner, but she didn't think it was a good idea to use it. Adjusting the desk lamp, she used the camera function on her cellphone and sent the image to Colonel Stockwell.

Charity had gone up to the restaurant because she was hungry. She hadn't eaten since her late-afternoon sandwich the day before, and now her hunger was mounting. Grabbing her purse, she went to her backpack and retrieved her Sig. *From now on*, she thought, as she slid the weapon into the purse, *I'll be armed everywhere I go.*

Without another thought, she left the room and took the elevator back up to the rooftop restaurant. Before the elevator reached the top, her phone chimed, alerting her to an incoming message.

> *Subject is Victor Pitt, former clandestine asset with the Agency. Disappeared six years ago, whereabouts unknown. He has knowledge that is considered dangerous to the Agency, but not a threat to your mission. Proceed as you think best.*

Charity pushed the phone back into her purse and had her hand on the Sig when the doors opened. Rene was standing there, waiting for the elevator. The two collegiate clowns were gone.

Charity smiled. "Looks like I'm the one holding the gun this time, Victor. Let's go back to our table."

He started to reach for his pocket and Charity leveled the Sig inside her purse, thumbing the hammer back. The sound froze him in place.

"I'm hungry, Victor, and you interrupted my breakfast. So now you're buying my breakfast while you tell me all about what a bad boy you've been. Move."

He turned slowly, then walked toward the table by the railing. Charity gave him three steps, then followed. She waited a few feet away until he sat down, then took the chair directly across from him, her hand never leaving her purse.

The waiter came and poured coffee as the two stared at each other. Charity ordered a bacon and cheese omelet and the waiter left the table.

"I was wrong," Rene said. "What I took for poor field craft was simple disinterest. How did you come up with my name so fast?"

Slowly, Charity released her grip on the pistol and pulled the sketch from her purse. "Relax, Rene. I said I wasn't here for you, and I'm not."

He looked down at the sketch and then smiled up at Charity. "I must have made a pretty good impression."

"Somewhat," she replied. "But don't flatter yourself. I'm just good with pencil and paper. Look, I've been instructed to proceed any way I see fit, where you are concerned."

"And just how do you see fit?"

"I have a few questions first," Charity replied. "I know who you are and what you used to be. I know when you quit and disappeared. I know you've been a boat builder and now do odd jobs on boats. Or at least that's what your background shows. What I don't know is why."

"Why I left?"

Charity nodded.

Rene looped his left arm over the rail and turned in his chair slightly, pushing his legs out in a relaxed pose. "I bet you could find out anyway—and what you'd find out will be a lie, more than likely."

Charity waited, saying nothing—a tactic she'd learned from McDermitt during their boat ride back to civilization. The man was a good listener and made people want to talk without saying or doing a thing.

Rene sighed. "It was six years ago this fall."

The significance meant a lot to Charity. She'd participated in the summer Olympics in Sydney just a year before that, earning a bronze medal in the women's four-hundred-meter medley. At twenty-five, she'd been one of the older members on the Olympic swim team, but was determined to be part of the games in Athens three years later. Then the planes hit the towers and changed everything.

"Nine-Eleven?"

Rene nodded somberly. "I was in Frisco. My fiancée was flying in from Newark. We were gonna be married the next day."

"Flight Ninety-Three?"

His eyes fixed on hers for a moment. She could see the hurt, and felt his pain. "Yeah," he said with a heavy sigh. "She called me after the plane had been taken. Just like everyone else, I figured it was a hijack for hostages or ransom. Then reports started coming in about the Twin Towers and the Pentagon. I tried to call her back, but kept getting her voicemail. Then I heard that Ninety-Three went down in a field in Pennsylvania."

"I'm sorry, Rene."

"Ancient history," he said. Though he shrugged it off, Charity could see the torment in his eyes. "I never went back to Langley after that. I bought a boat in Frisco and sailed south. Spent the winter in Cabo San Lucas, mostly in a drunken stupor. By the following summer, I'd wound up in Panama. That's where the first attempt was made."

"First attempt?" Charity asked.

"There've been three attempts to kill me so far," he replied. "The second was in Belize, three years ago. Then in Puerto Rico last year."

"What happened to them?"

"No idea," Rene replied. "I disappeared. Something I'm very good at. When you showed up here, after bumping into you in the Caymans, I was certain this was the fourth attempt by the Agency to kill me. Had you not come up in that elevator when you did, you would never have seen me again."

"Why do they want you dead?"

"Dead or back in the fold. I know things that could bury quite a few people way above both our pay grades. They kept me in line and silent with vague threats toward Alecia. I knew how the game was played in the Puzzle Palace. But once she was gone, there wasn't anything holding me. So I disappeared."

"And you've been on the run for six years? Always looking over your shoulder?"

"It's not as bad as it sounds. In most of the places I find myself, anyone like me sticks out like a sore thumb."

Charity considered what he'd said and decided he was telling the truth. "You have nothing to worry about where I'm concerned. I'll be finished here in a few days and flying back to my boat in the Caymans."

"Just what a good field agent would say to throw me off."

Charity smiled. "If it weren't true, you'd have been dead the second the elevator doors opened. You're not the only one who can disappear."

Rene slowly nodded. "Yes, I suppose that's true. Where do we go from here?"

"For now," Charity said with a wicked smile, "take me to this mango festival. Later, we can decide on where to go from there, your room or mine."

CHAPTER TWENTY-FOUR:

"What is a helicopter doing out here?" Martin Beisch asked. "Most of our people have never even seen one."

"We still do not know," Leon replied. "After it left here, it continued upriver. Karl saw it while he was inspecting the old man's farm yesterday afternoon."

The babo looked up from his desk. "What happened there?"

"He said he shot it," Himmel replied. "But it must be armored, because it flew away."

"Or he missed," Beisch said, rising from behind his desk and walking to the window. "I meant what happened with the old man?"

"Both he and the other farmer are growing coca. The *botaniker* confirmed that what they are growing came from his modified seeds. He predicts they can harvest well before the flood."

Beisch's back was to Himmel, as he gazed through the window at the many homes and shops that made up their community. "Tell Karl I wish to inspect the wall. As soon as possible."

"Right away. Will there be anything else?"

"No, that is all."

Without another word, Leon left Beisch's office. A young boy waited in the foyer of the large house. There were more than a dozen such boys, whose only purpose was to move quickly from one part of the community to another, delivering messages.

"Find Aleksander," Leon told the boy. "Tell him to report to the babo at once. Then go to the farm and alert Wirth that the babo will be inspecting the wall this morning."

The boy dashed out the door. In seconds, he'd disappeared down the foot path that connected all the buildings in the commune. They'd once used battery-powered radios to communicate with the outlying parts of the community, but Beisch had put a stop to it, thinking that with civilization pushing its way up the river others might hear them.

The boy found Karl quite easily. Almost out of breath, he told the man that the babo wanted to inspect the wall right away, and he'd been told to continue there to let Wirth know.

"No need of that," Karl said. "Go ahead and take your break here. Wirth is always ready."

The truth was, Wirth was very busy this time of year and the field beyond the wall was usually neglected as a result. It would do the man good to have the babo yank his chain. Then Karl could step in and take charge personally, sending Wirth and his men through the door in the wall to the other side, giving him some time alone with Jenifer.

Karl crossed his small yard and entered his workshop. His position allowed him a few modern provisions that others in the community would like to have, but that their station didn't warrant. Inside the shop was where he kept his two all-terrain vehicles. One was the standard ATV, with racks mounted front and rear for carrying loads, and two seats like a motorcycle. The other was larger, with side-by-side seating, a large cargo bed, and a roof with roll bars.

He climbed into the larger machine and started the engine, then went to the front of the shop and opened the two large doors. A moment later, Karl was moving down the path that took him from his home toward the big house on the point.

Babo was waiting on the porch, talking to Leon, when Karl brought the machine to a stop in the yard. He said something to Leon that Karl couldn't hear, then came down the steps and climbed into the passenger seat. In moments they were off.

"Is there anything else you would like to see, besides the wall?" Karl asked, after a few moments.

Ignoring the question, the babo said, "Leon told me that you shot at the helicopter."

Karl thought for only a second before answering. "I shot it, yes. But it must have some sort of steel hull, like the tanks our grandfathers drove."

Both men's paternal grandfathers had been tank commanders in the war. They'd deserted when it was obvious that Hitler's days were numbered, and came here with several other like-minded people. Both Karl and the babo had heard stories from their grandfathers about how thick the tank hulls were, and how bullets were ineffective against them.

"You *shot* the helicopter," Beisch conceded. "But your bullets did nothing. Why did you shoot at it?"

Karl glanced over at the leader of the small community, unsure of how to answer. Over the years, a handful of residents had left the jungle to see what life was like on the outside. At least that was the story that was usually circulated. While some did manage to find a way to leave the jungle, most had been dissidents that the former babo had culled.

Karl knew there were bones scattered on the bottom for half a mile downriver from the pier. He'd thrown quite a few men and several women from the pier himself. He and his men took turns with the women first. The new babo was even less tolerant of those who went against the community's standards of purity and harmony—purity of the people's pedigrees, and blind obedience to the wishes of the collective. The wishes of the collective were whatever the leader deemed necessary. It was the goal of the community to produce a pure and hearty population, a notion left behind by their grandfathers.

"My orders in a situation like that are clear, sir," Karl replied, after only a moment's hesitation. "Protect the *Bürger* from outsiders at any cost. I considered the helicopter to be a threat to our way of life."

"Yet, the man flying it has gotten away and probably reported the incident."

It was still several kilometers to the southern end of the community, where the wall separated it from the rest of the island. Karl drove in silence for a moment, not sure what to say. He didn't want to end up with his bones scattered on the bottom of the river.

The babo surprised him when he said, "Perhaps you need something more powerful than a rifle."

The trail narrowed as the last of the outpost buildings fell behind them. A few minutes later, Karl guided the machine into a small clearing surrounded by simple but sturdy homes. Each was elevated, sitting on stilts two meters off the ground.

All the people who lived here were busy in the fields at this hour, only a few within sight. The crops needed constant attention to keep them from being swallowed up by the fast growing jungle surrounding the fields on three sides.

"Go that way," Beisch said, pointing to the closer eastern shore. "Take me to where the wall meets the river, so I may check its effectiveness."

Turning the machine, Karl caught a glimpse of Jenifer coming out of the field, her father right behind her. He smiled inwardly. The babo was both respected and feared by everyone. *And here I am with the leader*, Karl thought.

The all-wheel-drive machine had no trouble with the mud near the bank of the river. Karl guided it expertly through the soft, loamy earth, bouncing over occasional ruts and dead branches that had floated up with the last flood. In a few months, the fields would be harvested, and everything around them would be underwater. The farmers' homes were built high above the ground, protected from the annual floodwaters. The homes and shops of the main body of the community were clustered tightly together on much higher ground at the northern tip of the island.

Stopping the machine at the end of the wall, he turned off the engine. The only sounds were the ticking of the exhaust as the engine cooled, and an occasional cry from a bird or animal on the other side of the river.

Beisch dismounted, his knee-high boots protecting his pants from the mud as he trudged to the waterline. Karl followed at a respectful distance. Beisch stopped at the base of the wall, which towered nearly four meters above their heads.

Knowing how the wall was constructed, it was hard for Karl to not laugh as the babo placed both hands against the wall and tried to push. The wood was very dense, and each plank in the wall was set deep into the ground. For more than sixty years, the annual floodwaters had pushed against the wall with tremendous power. Never once had any part of it failed or been undermined.

Beisch turned and walked along the wall, motioning Karl to follow. "How many of your men are posted out here?"

"Two men stand guard throughout the night during the summer months," Karl replied, pointing ahead of them to a ladder and platform mounted to the wall. "Each man has his own stand, from which they can see any movement on the other side. They sleep during the day, while two of the field hands usually take their places."

Indeed, there was a man standing on the nearest platform. Yet the other one, more than a kilometer away, appeared empty. "Two farmers?" the babo asked.

Just then, Erik Wirth emerged from between two rows of tall corn. Breathing hard from exertion, Wirth approached the babo. "Herr Beisch," Wirth said, grunting the words out. "I was not informed you were coming out here today."

"That is quite apparent!" Beisch roared. "Why do you have only one man on lookout?"

Looking flustered, Wirth started to say something, when Jenifer came out of the corn rows, her hair competing with the corn silk for brightness—and winning easily.

Karl interrupted Wirth as his daughter approached. "One man is enough during the day, sir. Erik's men are better suited to working the fields."

Wirth glared at Karl, surprised at the man coming to his defense, and hating that he did so. "Yes, one man is enough. A second man can be added in a matter of seconds if needed. Nothing has ever gotten through the field, much less scaled the wall. One man can cover the field beyond quite effectively."

Beisch turned to Karl. "Is this right?"

"Yes, sir. Erik was on the other side of the field when we came this way and he arrived here in moments. Many of his men were much closer." Pointing to the elevated platform, Karl continued. "If that man up there sounded an alarm, a second man would be in the other stand in a matter of seconds. If need be, more will be at the door, ready for anything."

"What is the status of the field beyond the wall?" Beisch asked, pleasing Karl to no end. He knew what it looked like; he'd just seen it yesterday.

"I am afraid it gets a bit neglected, this time of year," Wirth replied.

"Bring the machine, Karl," the babo said. "We will have a look."

Karl nodded at Jenifer and winked, before running back to where the large ATV sat. Jumping in, he started it and returned to the others.

"Get on the back," Beisch ordered Wirth, as he climbed in.

The man and his daughter took the rear facing seat in the cargo box, as Karl gunned the engine and steered toward the only break in the wall. Once there, the four of them dismounted, Beisch walking straight toward the large door. It was more than a meter wide and nearly two and a half meters tall. Wirth quickly joined him, as Karl and Jenifer stayed by the machine.

"Open it," the babo ordered.

Erik removed the hefty wooden timber that held the door tightly in place and set it aside. He pushed the heavy door open with his shoulder, and the two men disappeared through it.

Jenifer started to follow after them, but Karl put a hand on her shoulder. "Better if you wait here," Karl said, removing his hat. "You look beautiful, as always."

Her face colored slightly at the older man's compliment. Though they were scheduled to be married in just a few months, the hand on her shoulder was the first physical contact the two had ever had.

"Why is the babo here?" Jenifer asked.

"The flying machine yesterday has him worried," Karl replied, unsure if she knew what a helicopter was.

"I saw it," she said, as Karl took a step closer. "I had heard stories of such things, but have never seen one. The babo seems to rely on you very much."

Unintelligible shouting could be heard from beyond the wall. A moment later, Wirth came through the door looking flushed, Beisch right behind him.

"Karl!" the babo shouted at him. "The far field looks deplorable! A man could walk across it in a crouch and not be seen. Send every available man through there and get that corrected!"

Wirth was already shouting orders to the men in the field. Jenifer started to follow them through the door, but the babo stopped her. "This is men's work, child. You stay here." Then Beisch turned to Karl, a knowing look on his face. "Keep the women and children working in the field, Karl. I will direct the men personally."

Beisch followed the last of the men through the door and closed it behind them. Orders were shouted, though the wall was too dense and too high to make out what any of them were saying. Jenifer started to turn back toward the field, and Karl stopped her with a hand on her shoulder again.

"The other women know what to do," he said. Reaching out and putting his hands on her narrow waist, he drew her closer to him. "We will be husband and wife in just a few months. I think it is time we got to know each other a little better."

CHAPTER TWENTY-FIVE:

When Napier woke up, it was already light out. The Fleming woman—and he was sure that wasn't her real name—had dropped him off at his house the previous afternoon before flying back across the mountains to the airport. She'd given the boat a cursory inspection, leaving him with instructions to have it in the water and ready by tomorrow morning.

The woman's flying scared the hell out of Thurman, even though he'd flown in choppers in combat situations before. It wasn't so much her flying that scared him. There hadn't been a second when she didn't seem to be in complete and total control. It was more about her calculated coldness at the controls. If the chopper had had guns mounted on it, Aleksander would have been opened up like a ripe melon before he could have shouldered the rifle. That much, Napier was sure of.

At times, it had seemed like she was two different people. The cold and calculating one seemed to be in control most of the time. But just below the surface Thurman sensed a cauldron of emotion that seemed ready to explode without warning. That was what scared him. When it happened, and he was certain it would, he didn't want to be anywhere around her.

He'd spent the rest of the evening checking the boat over very closely, and thinking. He filled the gas tanks and inspected fluid levels. The engines were new; the tachometers barely moved when the keys were turned on, indicating almost no hours on the engines. He'd drained a small amount of oil from each engine's crankcase and filtered it through a coffee filter, expecting to find minute metal shavings, but there weren't any.

Once he'd finished his inspection, he'd driven down to one of his favorite waterfront dives, where he nursed a brace of beers while thinking about what this trip upriver might bring. By the time the bar closed, he'd all but made up his mind to tell Stockwell to come and get the boat, he wanted no part of this.

The new bartender, a young island woman named Jade, was also one of the Trinidad's better-looking prostitutes. He'd offered her a hundred dollars to come back to his house with him and spend the night. She'd jumped at his proposition immediately. A hundred bucks was a lot of money here, but was nothing to Thurman.

She wasn't in the bed, so Thurman got up and walked naked into the next room, looking for her. From the kitchen, he heard a quiet voice singing an island melody.

Hearing him approach, Jade turned to face him. "Yuh want breakfast, yuh go put on some clothes."

"How 'bout I just eat you for breakfast?" he grumbled, sniffing the air like a bear. He didn't know what he had in the kitchen to cook, but something smelled good.

Jade looked him up and down, lingering on his manhood for only a moment. "Yuh done had 'nuff a dat cyat last night. Me? I'm hungry for some real food, dis morning."

Thurman went back to the bedroom and scrounged around in a dresser for a clean pair of shorts, then returned to the kitchen, pulling them up as he came up behind her. "I didn't know there was any food here."

"Jest some canned meat," she replied, cracking eggs into a mixing bowl. "And yuh birds provide a few eggs. Yuh take me home after we eat?"

He sat down at one of the two chairs by the small table and watched her as she worked at the stove. She wore a pair of cut-off jeans and a bikini top, standard island attire.

A tiny wisp of a woman, Jade had plenty of curves in all the right places and cocoa-colored skin, only slightly darker than his own weathered complexion. In the States, she'd have been considered an exotic beauty. At barely five feet tall, the top of her head barely reached the middle of Thurman's chest.

"I'm headed down there in a coupla hours," he replied. "Gotta deliver a boat."

Tossing her long black hair over her shoulder, Jade looked back at him. "Coupla hours? More bull gonna cost yuh more money, Mister Cyclops."

Thurman didn't mind the nickname, particularly from a woman he'd tossed around on his big bed the night before. "You know I'm good for it, baby."

She smiled broadly at the prospect of even more money, then placed two plates on the table. "Yuh eat first, Uncle. Big ole bull gwon need more energy for di next round. Jade not gwon be easy on yuh, dis time."

She sat down next to Thurman, and they both ate quickly. When she was finished, Jade left the dishes on the table and disappeared into the bedroom.

When she returned, she had the big blanket from Thurman's bed rolled up under one arm. She grabbed his hand, leading him to the front door. "I wanna do it outside," she said. "More room."

With one hand, Thurman scooped her up over his shoulder and carried her toward the front door.

"Put me down!" she yelled, as he ducked to get through the door and out into the sunlight. "I don like being up dis high."

He shifted her body around. Bringing her down in front of him, but not letting her feet touch the ground, Thurman cupped her ass in his two huge hands. Jade squealed and wrapped her legs around his waist and her arms around his thick neck, nibbling and biting at his shoulder. As she started grinding her body against him, moans and squeaks escaped her, and Thurman carried her out onto the grassy lawn on the side of the house.

Dropping the blanket, Jade arched her back, clasping her fingers around Thurman's neck and rocking her hips against his. He put one arm around her tiny waist and held her there, as she arched back even more, releasing her hold on his neck. With his other hand, Thurman pulled the strings of her bikini top and let it fall away, massaging her breasts. Jade pulled him deeper with her legs, spurring him like a wild bronco as she rode him in a nearly inverted position.

Arching her back even more, Jade stretched her arms out to the ground. With her palms flat on the grass and her hips thrusting against him with wild abandon, she moaned loudly as her whole body quivered.

Thurman lowered her to the ground, where she moved her body around, spreading the blanket under her. Standing over her, Thurman said, "Damn, girl. You coulda waited till we at least got our pants off."

An hour later, the two of them lay side by side on the blanket, both their bodies glistening with sweat in the mid-morning sunlight. *She wasn't lying*, he thought, his chest heaving to get more air to his oxygen-deprived lungs.

"You *were* going easy on me last night."

"Dat's what I say," Jade replied with an impish grin as she reached over and fondled him. "Old bull can't come charging outa di gate all at once. He gotta go slow di first few times."

Thurman chuckled, then struggled to his feet. "Let's get dressed, then you can help me hook up the boat."

Jade was on her feet quickly, picking up the blanket and shaking the dirt and grass off it. Seeing that Thurman was still somewhat unsteady on his feet, she picked up his shorts and tossed them to him.

"Yuh can feed me again, when we get to town," she said, wiggling to get her cutoffs up over her wide hips. She looked around the yard. "What boat?"

Thurman pointed toward the old hangar with his chin, as he stepped into his shorts. "It's in there."

Tossing the blanket over the rail on the side of the porch, Jade started that way, not bothering to put on her bikini top. "Show mi dis boat."

Thurman caught up to her and muscled the big hangar door to the side, the old, rusty wheels squeaking in protest.

"Dem old wheels like di Cyclops," Jade said stepping into the hot, humid air inside the hangar. "Dey jest need a little grease, to get to moving easy." As Thurman pushed the other door open, Jade went to the boat, walking along the side and tracing her hand along the sleek black hull. "What a boat like dis for?"

"A guy gave it to me," Thurman said. "In exchange for taking some psycho up the Manamo."

"Is a pretty boat," Jade said, stepping up onto the trailer fender.

"Go ahead and climb in, if you want."

She scampered over the gunwale, landing lightly in bare feet on the deck by the console. "Yuh say yuh taking it back? Why yuh not keepin' it?"

Though she was standing on the boat's deck, she was only a few inches above eye level with him. With her hands on her hips, her feet apart, and her pert breasts pointing toward the hangar's rafters, Thurman had a vision of being out on the water with this beautiful little woman.

"What I'd have to do to keep it is too dangerous," he said, climbing aboard.

"Ha! Too dangerous for di Cyclops? I seen yuh take on four men, all of dem much younger dan yuh. What so dangerous 'bout goin' up di river?"

Not seeing any harm in telling her, Thurman replied, "I'd have to take some crazy woman up there to kill the babo."

The fear in Jade's eyes was clearly visible. "Kill di babo? How can yuh kill someting dat cannot be killed?"

"Good question," Thurman said, sitting down on the forward bench seat and pulling her onto his lap. "And I got no idea."

"Boat like dis," Jade said, smiling and squirming around to get comfortable, "could be a lot of fun down dere in town. And all yuh gotta do is take dis woman up di river? How dat be dangerous to di Cyclops?"

Thurman considered the question, as Jade tugged at the button on his shorts, freeing and slowly stroking his member. "Another good question," he moaned, as she knelt down on the deck between his knees.

CHAPTER TWENTY-SIX:

ravis Stockwell pulled his SUV into the little marina at the foot of the bridge to No Name Key and parked. The charter fishing boat he was meeting was just entering the basin, its sleek black hull shining in the early morning sunlight. He climbed out and grabbing a small bag from the back, proceeded down to the dock.

Stockwell had announced his retirement months earlier and taken a job as first mate aboard this boat. It had all been a ruse, though. To act as Charity's handler, he needed to disassociate himself from the power brokers in DC.

Just as the boat bumped the fuel dock, Pescador, the big black dog in the cockpit, lifted his shaggy head and barked a greeting. Travis stepped aboard and the man at the helm reversed the port engine, expertly spinning the boat away from the dock and turning back toward the entrance.

Quickly stowing his go-bag in the salon, Travis went up the ladder to the bridge. "What the hell's going on down in Key West that you gotta drop everything and go down there all of a sudden?"

"Just meeting someone," Jesse McDermitt replied. "Might be an overnighter. Glad you brought your bag."

Since his faked retirement, Stockwell had been working as McDermitt's first mate aboard *Gaspar's Revenge*, a luxury offshore fishing boat. The job was just a cover, providing Stockwell with time and proximity to support Charity on her missions. For McDermitt, the charter business was sort of a cover, as well. The man didn't need to work; he was worth millions. When needed he provided reliable transportation for Homeland Security's Caribbean Counter-terrorism Command.

Stockwell sat down in the starboard seat and looked at the big man at the helm curiously. "Come on, Jesse. You don't need me along just to visit someone in Key West. What gives?"

McDermitt gave him the rundown on what had happened the previous day at the *Rusty Anchor*, a local watering hole in Marathon. The story involved some cocaine dealer named Bradley and a kid who'd stolen from him.

When McDermitt finished, Travis thought about it for a moment. "What makes you think you can do anything to help this kid and why would you even want to help someone who ripped off a coke dealer in the first place?"

McDermitt ignored him while he turned the big boat into Bogie Channel and brought it up on plane, steering southeast into Spanish Harbor, navigating by sight. He had the latest in state-of-the-art navigation equipment, but knew the waters of the Middle Keys so well he rarely used any of it. Ahead were the two bridges spanning the narrow channel between Scout Key and Big Pine Key.

Once clear of the bridges, McDermitt pushed the throttles up to forty knots and started a wide, sweeping turn to the southwest.

"I don't know that I can help him," McDermitt finally replied. "But last night I looked up this Bradley guy on the Internet and saw a picture of him with someone else. His accountant, a guy named Chase Conner."

Travis scratched the side of his face, thinking. "I know I've heard the name. How do I know him?"

"You don't, but I do. Deuce may have mentioned him to you. He was the guy that bugged my boat last year and put everything into motion that cost a lot of people their lives and ended up with Doc taking a bullet in the back protecting me, not to mention getting my boat blown up."

Deuce Livingston was currently filling Stockwell's seat in DC, furthering the subterfuge that Stockwell had retired to work as first mate for McDermitt, a job once held by Bob "Doc" Talbot, a former Navy Corpsman.

"Ah, so you're seeking retribution," Travis said.

"Yeah, something like that. If the opportunity arises. I'm going to pretend to be a big-time drug dealer, shake the trees and see what kind of rats fall out. I had Chyrel create a phony identity for me."

Stockwell's expression remained unchanged, pretending he hadn't been in contact with the group's IT guru since his so-called retirement. "When did you speak to her? How's she doing?"

"I video-conferenced with her last night. She was at home in Homestead. Seems to be doing okay."

The men rode in silence for several minutes, before McDermitt said, "Take the wheel, Travis. I gotta learn who I am."

Switching seats, McDermitt put his feet up on the console, opened the file and started to read the fake bio. The whole thing was news to Stockwell, though Deuce was still keeping him in the loop and he was still the one calling the shots. He'd spoken with Miss Koshinski just two days ago, as well.

After a while, McDermitt closed the folder and said, "While we're down there, I'll be Stretch Buchannan, a medium-level cocaine distributor out of Key Largo. You're my bodyguard and we're down there to check out someone nosing into my distribution territory."

"This GT Bradley?" Stockwell asked. If Chyrel knew something and hadn't passed the information on to him, he wanted to get to the bottom of it. But he also didn't want to allow his true status to get out. He knew McDermitt pretty well, and was sure that he could be trusted, but now wasn't the time to tell him anything about Charity's mission.

Careful where you step, Stockwell thought.

McDermitt handed him a printout with a picture of two men, obviously taken from a newspaper headline. "That's Bradley on the left," McDermitt said. "And his chauffeur, Erik Lowery. The guy behind them is Chase Conner."

"You sure? His face is only partly in the picture and a little out of focus."

"It's him," McDermitt replied.

"And he's in Key West, too?"

"No, I don't think so. But if I can swing it, it'd sure be nice to find out exactly where he is."

Travis looked straight ahead, glancing at the photo to commit it to memory. He handed it back to McDermitt, who continued to read the fake background Chyrel had created for him.

Finally, Travis broke the silence. "I still don't understand why you wanted me along."

McDermitt stowed the folder. "My relationship with Deuce goes back a long way. I've known the guy since he was a kid. His dad and I were friends."

Stockwell glanced over at McDermitt, holding his gaze. At first his eyes were intense, as if McDermitt had struck a nerve. Travis forced a neutral expression. "You've totally lost me now, Jesse."

"Deuce was raised by a Marine, and he's a SEAL," McDermitt said, an edge to his voice. "There's more honor in that man than anyone else I know, *Colonel*."

McDermitt hadn't called him that since Stockwell had stepped down from his position as associate secretary. Stockwell's jaw muscles contracted as he stared straight ahead.

"What exactly did you and Miss Koshinski talk about last night?" Stockwell asked, trying but failing to hide the irritation in his voice.

"Her orders were clear," McDermitt replied. "You don't have to worry. She's a team player all the way. But I don't like being lied to, especially by people I consider a friend."

Stockwell dropped the façade, knowing that Jesse had probably figured out a thing or two. In a more official tone, he said, "Above your paygrade, Jesse."

"Switch seats," McDermitt ordered and stood up.

Stockwell obliged, and once the captain was back at the helm, he slowly pulled back on the throttles, bringing the *Revenge* down to idle speed just inside the reef line, west of American Shoal. Travis noted that they were a good three miles from shore.

Turning to Travis, Jesse studied the side of his face. "Bullshit, Colonel. I haven't had a paygrade in over eight years now. I don't give a hairy rat's ass whose idea it was, but making Deuce lie to his friends goes completely contrary to his sense of honor. You can spout national security all you want, but I know it's about control, and you're not the controlling type. But Deuce would never jeopardize the security of this country, and if he were ordered not to divulge something, he wouldn't. That forces him to lie, which is so against his nature, he'd alienate himself from his friends, pretty much like he's doing now. Tell me I'm off base."

Travis looked starboard, toward the distant shore. "Chyrel's good. No doubt she picked up some intel she wasn't supposed to and passed it on to you. That's not good."

Glancing over, McDermitt seemed almost relieved at what Stockwell said. "Chyrel's one of the good ones. If it's even implied that something should be kept secret, she wouldn't spill. She told me straight up she wasn't allowed to talk to me about anything job-related. Just because I'm a grunt doesn't mean I can't add two and two, Colonel. You've been lying to me all along. And spying on me. I never mentioned Bradley's first name."

Stockwell turned quickly toward his friend and started to say something.

"Please don't compound that lie with a lie of denial," McDermitt interrupted. "There's no investigation going on into Charity's disappearance. That means she's on the company clock. If you even attempt to deny it, you'll swim to shore from here."

Stockwell involuntarily tightened his grip on the armrests of the chair. He wasn't a man accustomed to being dressed down and felt like a wet-behind-the-ears lieutenant that he'd made such a blunder. After a moment, he relaxed and sighed. "It was just a matter of time until you and the other team members put it together."

"She's doing wet work for the DHS and you're her handler?"

"No, not DHS," Stockwell replied vaguely, looking off toward shore once more.

"You're shittin' me! The CIA?"

Stockwell turned toward the man he considered a friend. He'd hoped the truth wouldn't come out quite so soon, but known that it would sooner or later. "You didn't hear it from me."

"And Deuce knows, but was ordered to keep it under his hat?"

Lowering his head slightly, Stockwell replied, "Even his wife doesn't know."

The truth was that Deuce was in a situation where his duty had to be placed above his honor. Though he didn't like it one bit, Stockwell had indeed ordered the man to lie. The *Revenge* gently rocked in the swells, with the sun high above the eastern horizon. Gulls dove toward the stream of turbulent water at the stern as if expecting someone to throw fish guts overboard. Suddenly, McDermitt pushed the throttles to the stops and the big boat nearly leapt out of the water.

"Sometimes, Colonel," McDermitt began, obviously irritated, "A man's honor has to be placed above his duty. Maybe not with everyone. There are plenty out there whose sense of duty easily outweighs their sense of honor. Not with a man like Deuce, though. This has to be tearing at the very fabric of his being."

"You have to keep what you know to yourself, Jesse."

Turning in his seat, McDermitt gave Stockwell a threatening look. "Like hell I do, *Director*. Don't worry, I won't be shouting it from the rooftops, but there are people in the man's life that have a right to know. People in Charity's life, too. Their friends and family. Deuce can't function at a hundred percent with a lie to his wife hanging over his head."

"This is why you brought me along? So you could threaten to feed me to the sharks if I didn't divulge a matter of national security? What Charity's doing down there is important, and she's good at it."

"I've no doubt she is," McDermitt said. "I've seen her work up close. With your predecessor." He seemed to relax after a moment and pulled back on the throttles, slowing the boat but not coming down off plane. "Truth is, I do need you, Travis. These guys in Key West are dangerous."

Stockwell knew full well the kind of man McDermitt was, and he also knew that he could trust the man's judgment. He grinned at Jesse and said, "Then let's go see the fortune teller. We can figure the other problem out later, all right?"

CHAPTER TWENTY-SEVEN:

When Charity woke the next morning, Rene was gone. How he'd slipped out of her bed without waking her was a mystery. She struggled to free herself from the disheveled sheets and blanket.

When she rose, she found two of the pillows on the floor, along with her faded yellow tee-shirt. Picking it up, she pulled it over her head, tossing her hair and pulling the shirt down over her hips before stepping through the open glass doors and onto the balcony.

"Good morning," Rene said, startling her. He was seated in the corner, hidden by the partially closed drapes inside.

"I thought you'd left," Charity said, looking away from him and out over the water below.

"Considered it," he replied, standing and moving to the rail beside her. "But I thought it'd seem kinda cheap and tawdry."

A gust of wind blew Charity's hair across her face. She managed to tuck most of it behind her ear, but a few strands escaped her as she turned her head to face him. "So you're not the slam-bam-thank-you-ma'am type?" she asked with a smile.

"Hardly," Rene replied with a chuckle. "What are your plans today? Or will you have to kill me, if you tell me?"

Charity considered the question. Having an extra pair of eyes would be a benefit and Rene, being someone trained to observe and remember, would be far better than the one-eyed giant she'd taken upriver yesterday.

"I want to fly upriver again," she replied, reaching a decision. "There's a man up there I need to talk to. Would you care to tag along?"

"Up the Manamo?" Rene asked. Charity nodded and he considered it for a moment. "Yeah, I could do that. I don't leave for a couple of days."

"Good," Charity said, turning and clasping her fingers behind his neck. Rene slid into her embrace, the surprise in his eyes evident when his hands found only her bare back and bottom.

Charity leaned in and kissed him. Not a deep, passionate kiss like the night before, but not a quick peck, either.

Rene drew her closer and she whispered in his ear, "I need a shower, coffee, and food, in that order." Then she pushed him back slightly. "Neither of us slept much last night."

"You mean that really happened? I thought I was dreaming."

She smiled, remembering how much they'd had to drink at the festival and how for a few hours, she'd been just a woman enjoying life and having fun with a man.

"If it was a dream, it was an exhausting one," she said.

"I'll meet you up there. I need a shower myself."

"The shower's big enough for two here," Charity said, then gave him a wicked smile. "And there's a hot tub."

Two hours later, with the sun already halfway up the morning sky, Charity and Rene stepped out of the elevator in the lobby. She stopped at the concierge's desk and asked if there was a package for her and the man disappeared into a room behind the desk. He returned with a small box, which she signed for and stuffed into her backpack. Outside, she started toward the lone taxi waiting by the entrance, but Rene put a hand on her shoulder.

"We can take my scooter," he offered, nodding toward a row of rental scooters and bikes. "It's just over there."

Once he got the little machine started, Charity threw a leg over and climbed on behind him, wrapping her arms around his waist. The ride to the airport only took a couple of minutes. Rene pulled into the private aircraft terminal, parking the scooter under some trees in the corner of the lot.

Ten minutes later, they were airborne, climbing in a steep turn, banking to the left over the shore line. Charity glanced over at Rene. Unlike the man from the previous day, he was sitting comfortably, craning his neck slightly to look down at the people on the beach.

"Do you handle a boat as well as you do this Huey?" Rene asked over the intercom headset.

"Not yet," she replied. "I've been sailing and flying ever since I was a kid. More flying than sailing the last few years."

"Who's this guy you're going to meet?"

"I'm not sure. He's a farmer, is about all I know."

"You don't even know his name?" Rene asked, as Charity put the chopper into a shallow dive, heading towards the wave tops just beyond the southern tip of the island.

"No, but I think it's important that I talk with him."

A hundred feet above the water, Charity leveled off, pointing the nose of the chopper straight in the direction of the farm where the old man lived. *No messing around, flying along the river*, she thought. *Straight in, then maybe fly over that wall again on the way out.*

As they approached the mainland, the jungle canopy rose up from a deserted beach. Charity pulled back on the cyclic, bringing the bird up higher. Just like the day before, the jungle looked like something from some distant time, green and impenetrable as far as she could see.

"Beautiful," Rene said, as they soared over the desolate beach and the trees just beyond it.

"Not far removed from the primordial ooze our ancestors crawled out of," Charity remarked, remembering what Napier had said about the jungle.

"How far upriver is this farmer?"

"Not far," she replied, pointing to the GPS display on the dash. "I was there yesterday, but we flew along the river and it winds back and forth a lot."

"We?"

"My guide showed me the way."

Off to the right, the river could be seen whenever it twisted east or west from its mostly north-to-south course. It didn't take long at all before there were signs of civilization. A large swath of jungle opened up into a clear-cut area, laid out in haphazard grids.

Near the middle, a portion of the jungle remained, and Charity could see that there was a large clearing in the center of it that she'd missed yesterday.

Flying past the jungle oasis, she banked and looked past Rene at the clearing. It appeared to be plenty large enough to land in. Hopefully there wasn't any loose debris that might get whipped up into the rotors. As Charity circled back, she decided stealth was worth the risk, seeing nothing but grass in the clearing.

"You're going to land in there?" Rene asked, with a tinge of alarm in his voice.

Without answering, Charity pulled back on the cyclic, bleeding off speed as she banked even more to the right and increased power. Slowly, she leveled the Huey and carefully brought it down into the clearing, the chopper seeming to be swallowed up by the dense jungle around it.

When they were on the ground, Charity quickly shut down the turbine and moved aft, opening the storage locker. Reaching over, she pushed on the release catch and removed the tray full of camera equipment and set it aside.

"Are you armed?" she asked, looking up at Rene.

"I thought it would be wise," he replied, looking down into the false bottom of the storage locker at Charity's weapons. "But apparently not as well as you are."

She removed the sniper rifle and a second handgun, handing the Sig Sauer to Rene. "You can never be too well-armed."

Opening her backpack, she removed her own holstered Sig and clipped it onto her belt. Sliding open the cargo door, Charity quickly stepped down. When she turned toward the front of the chopper, a small man was standing just beyond the nose of the bird. He wore a long loincloth tied around his narrow waist and a faded Jimmy Buffett tee-shirt.

It was the old man she'd seen in her dreams, and again yesterday. He looked to be quite ancient, lines etching his face like a roadmap. His hair was long and mostly silver, his skin the color of Georgia clay. But it was his eyes that drew Charity's attention. Dark brown, clear, showing no fear, and full of wisdom.

"I am Vicente," he said. "Buyei of the Ye'kuana people."

Slinging the rifle over her left shoulder, Charity stepped closer to the old man, moving slowly so she wouldn't frighten him.

"My name is Charity Styleski," she said, using the name her great-grandfather had arrived in America with. She didn't know why she said it—her grandfather had changed it, dropping the *ki* before her father was born. The man's calming eyes inspired her to be completely open and honest.

"You are the wind dancer spirit," the old man replied, as Rene stepped up to join her.

She remembered suddenly her first dream about this man, and subsequent dreams about this place. As she slowly looked around the clearing, everything seemed familiar. Near the tree line, she saw two young boys hiding. She'd forgotten that first dream, where the old man had stood on the deck of her boat and she told him its name.

"Yes," she said with a smile. "I am *Wind Dancer*."

CHAPTER
TWENTY-EIGHT:

"Did you hear that?" Karl asked, not really expecting an answer.

"Hear what?" Jenifer said, finally pulling away from him, thankful for any distraction. "We will be married soon, Karl. We have to wait until then."

Karl turned, putting a hand behind his ear. Far in the distance, he heard the same whumping sound he'd heard before the helicopter came around the bend in the river. This time the sound was softer, and steady. It seemed to emanate from the jungle, far beyond the river to the east.

"It is the helicopter," Karl said, in a voice so low nobody could hear it.

Jogging quickly to the door in the wall, Karl pushed it open with his shoulder and stepped through. The farmers were scattered all through the huge field to the south, some swinging scythes and axes to cut back the jungle plants. Others were piling the cut leaves, branches, vines, and deadfalls into piles, two of which were already blazing.

As Karl approached him, the babo turned toward him. "It should never get like this, Karl. If Mister Wirth is unable to keep up with it during the harvest, your men will have to do it."

"I think the helicopter is returning," Karl said. "I could hear it, far off to the east."

The babo turned and took several steps toward the river, listening. But with the sounds of the men working, Karl knew he would not be able to hear it.

"Come to the other side," Karl said. "There is too much noise here."

The two men walked through the door and Karl pulled it closed. Jenifer had walked toward the river, and motioned them to follow. When they caught up to her, she was standing with her head cocked slightly, as if listening to something.

"It is very far away," Jenifer said. "I can only hear it now and then."

The two men listened. "I hear nothing," Beisch said.

Neither Karl nor Jenifer replied for a moment. Then Karl heard the helicopter again, the whumping growing louder as it had the previous day, but still far off to the southeast.

"There!" Karl said. "Do you hear it now?"

"Yes," Beisch replied, putting a hand to his chin, deep in thought.

The sound grew in intensity, becoming steady, but it still seemed very far off. After a moment, the whumping stopped. Karl waited a long minute, to see if he could hear it again, but all was silent. Stepping further away from the wall, Karl cupped a hand behind his ear again and waited, but the sound was gone.

"It landed," the babo said. "What is down there, where a helicopter can land?"

Turning toward Beisch and Jenifer, Karl replied, "The farms."

"Go get the boat!" Beisch shouted. "Bring two of your men and pick me up here."

Sprinting to the ATV, Karl climbed in and started the engine. Jamming the gear shifter into low, he stomped the throttle, spinning the rear tires and slinging mud as he turned toward the trailhead. He drove the machine as fast as possible back toward his home, and came sliding to a stop at the house next to his.

"Rolph!" Karl shouted at the house.

The door opened and Rolph Hoffman stepped out onto the porch, his young wife cowering behind him. "What is it, Erik?"

"Get one of the men! Anyone you can find quickly, and meet me at the pier."

As Hoffman started down the steps, Karl started the machine and raced across the yard separating the two homes. He stopped at his small shop and ran inside. Uncasing his rifle, he returned quickly to the machine and roared off again. A minute later, he was on the boat. After stowing the rifle, he quickly started the engine and untied the stern line from the dock. The current kept the boat in place.

Rolph came trotting down the dock, David Kohler right behind him. Rolph Hoffman was Karl's most trusted man, and Kohler one of the biggest in Karl's small security force.

"David, get the bow line!" Karl shouted, as Rolph stepped down into the boat.

"What is going on?" Rolph said. "Why the hurry?"

"The helicopter returned," Karl said, as Kohler pushed the bow away from the dock and leaped aboard. "It sounded as if it might have landed at one of the farms."

Karl engaged the transmission, turned the boat upriver, and accelerated. Minutes later, the boat rounded the bend in the river, and the wall came into view. Beisch was standing at the water's edge, hands on his hips.

Karl turned toward shore, slowing the boat until it nosed up on the bank next to the leader. The babo grabbed the low rail in both hands and vaulted upward, slinging his right leg over the rail, as his arms straightened, holding him high above the side of the boat.

Once the babo was onboard, Karl reversed the engine, catching a glimpse of Jenifer and her father standing by the wall, watching them. The girl smiled and waved as Karl backed away from the bank and turned the boat upriver. He nodded at her as he shifted the engine to forward and accelerated toward the farms.

Joining Karl at the helm, Beisch shouted over the screaming outboard, "If it landed at one of the farms, we should be able to see it from the river."

The first of the farms was twenty minutes away at full throttle. Karl knew that if the helicopter took off, they might not hear it over the engine. But getting there quickly was more important.

"Rolph, both of you be ready on the bow," Karl ordered. "If you see the black flying machine, shoot it down."

The two men quickly uncased their rifles and moved up onto the bow, taking a seat on either side with their rifles at the ready. Fifteen minutes later, just a mile from the first farm, the boat approached a narrow bend in the river. Karl heard the beating sound of the chopper before he saw it; before he could shout a warning, it roared around the bend, flying almost on its side before shooting past the boat. It all happened so quickly that neither man was able to get off a shot.

"Hang on!" Karl shouted, whipping the wheel toward the right bank. He then spun it the opposite way, turning the boat in a skid and throwing up a huge, arcing spray and rooster tail.

By the time the boat was turned and going downriver, the helicopter had disappeared around the next bend. Karl pushed the throttle all the way forward and gave chase.

"Get ready!" he shouted to the men up in the bow. "You might get only one shot!"

Karl angled across the river toward the point, cutting the distance to the long straight part of the river that he remembered was just around the bend. He knew the water would be shallower there, but trusted that there would be enough to keep the boat up on plane.

Turning just a few feet from the river bank, he saw the helicopter come into view. The boat was gaining on it as the two men opened fire.

Suddenly a huge crocodile surfaced just ahead and slightly to the right of the boat. Karl reacted instinctively, turning the wheel to avoid the large river predator, which could easily swamp the boat.

Just as they passed the croc, the hull made contact with one of the ever shifting sandbars, bringing the boat to a sudden stop. Karl quickly shifted into neutral and grabbed his own rifle, joining the men on the bow, who had both chambered a second round. Karl brought his rifle up, centering the scope's cross-hairs on the helicopter's exhaust, and all three fired in unison.

CHAPTER TWENTY-NINE:

"This is my friend, Rene," Charity said to the old man, who nodded a greeting.

"Please, come over to the shade and sit," Vicente said. "I have been expecting you."

Without waiting for a reply, he turned and started walking toward the two young men at the edge of the clearing. Charity and Rene joined him, both looking all around the clearing for any possible threat.

"You speak very good English," Rene said.

"I spent most of my youth working on a transport ship," Vicente said. "I speak English, Spanish, and German. I returned to my ancestral home twenty years ago, because I missed my people."

"You said you were the buyei of the Ye'kuana?" Charity asked, reaching the tree line. "What does that mean?"

Charity noticed that a trail disappeared just beyond the two boys. Vicente pointed up it and said something to one of the boys in his native tongue. The boy dashed off and was soon out of sight.

Vicente stood by the remnants of a small fire, and spread both hands. "Please, sit."

Rene looked at Charity and she nodded, moving to a spot near the old man. The three sat down and Vicente explained, "A buyei is what you would call a shaman or mystic. My father was buyei, as was his father before him. There are many different kinds of buyei, I am a healer and seer. My people, the Ye'kuana, are all but gone now. The name means Boat People, and for generations we lived on the rivers. Other tribes along the Manamo and Orinoco are interconnected in some way. The Ye'kuana, Warao, Pemon, Yanomami, we are all the children of Wanadi and the forest. I help the people in this area as best I can by providing medicine, advice, and spiritual healing."

The boy returned, carrying a small satchel which he handed to Vicente. From inside, the old man produced a hand-carved wooden pipe and a smaller bag.

"We will smoke to your arrival," he said, taking a small amount of yellowish-green powder and sprinkling it into the pipe's bowl. "This is the yopo seed. It allows one to see outside the world."

Leaning forward, the old man blew gently on the dead ashes in the fire pit. A tendril of smoke, then a flame, rose up from a twig. As he lifted the twig to his bowl, he sensed Charity's reluctance.

"Do not worry. The effect of the yopo seed will wear off in less than a minute with no harm. But it will seem to be a much longer time. During that minute, you may see, hear, and smell things that do not exist in this world. You may also converse with other spirits."

Vicente held the twig to the bowl and drew deeply. Then he waved the smoke from the bowl over his face and head and handed it to Charity. She took it and looked at the shaman questioningly.

"Fear not, Wind Dancer. It will not harm you."

Charity put the pipe to her lips and pulled, taking a small amount of smoke into her lungs. It tasted slightly acidic, with a tinge of bitterness. When she extended the pipe back to Vicente, he waved it toward Rene and she passed it to him.

Charity watched as Rene took a small puff, mimicking the old man, by waving the smoke over his head, before handing it back. When Charity looked back at Vicente, the lines in his face faded away and his hair seemed to change to the rich black color of the boys. All around them, the air seemed to darken and grow heavy.

Out of the darkness an apparition appeared, floating among the trees. As it descended to settle beside the old man, Charity recognized her by the clothes she wore. The same soft, tissue-thin garment the ancient woman in her dream had worn. Like Vicente, she appeared much younger now, full of vitality, but though she appeared to be standing next to the seated man, she was much smaller, not even at eye level to the seated man. Like his, her dark eyes spoke of the wisdom of eternity.

"You have come to help my people," the tiny apparition said, in a soft and soothing voice, with no discernible accent. "For that, I am very grateful. Vicente will guide you."

Before Charity could say anything, the woman's face seemed to disappear, as her whole body was engulfed in a hazy white smoke, drifting back up among the giant tree limbs. The air around them grew still and light. Then a few strands of hair, which had escaped Charity's pony-tail, were gently moved across her face by a light breeze.

Though Charity didn't remember saying anything, she sensed that she'd somehow had a long conversation with Vicente and the apparition.

"The Forest Mother is pleased," Vicente said, smiling softly. "You will recall more as time goes forward, and if you need my guidance you have only to ask."

The old man rose then—not like a man his age would normally stand, but with the ease of youth and strength. "You must go now. The babo is approaching."

Rene scrambled to his feet, extending a hand to Charity, which she took. "Hurry," the shaman urged. "You have only minutes before they discover you."

Realizing she hadn't said a word since smoking the pipe, Charity bowed her head to the old man, the lines in his face and his silver hair having returned to normal. "Will I see you again, Buyei?"

"Yes," he replied, smiling broadly. "But go quickly."

Rene and Charity trotted out to the middle of the clearing and quickly boarded the helicopter.

"What the hell was that all about?" Rene asked, strapping in and staring at the old man, now standing at the mouth of the trail.

Charity ignored the question, going through the starting sequence. In seconds, the turbine fired and she brought the rotors up to speed, raising the collective. The chopper lifted up from the ground and Charity pressed slightly on the right foot pedal, turning the bird toward the river.

At a hundred feet, she pulled in more power and pushed the cyclic forward, slowly accelerating away from the jungle clearing toward the river. Flying over what she assumed was Vicente's home, she turned downriver and brought the helicopter down close to the water.

"She was beautiful," Charity said. "And so tiny."

Rene's voice came over her headset. "Who?"

"The Forest Mother," Charity replied, looking over at Rene as she deftly guided the chopper around the first bend in the river.

"Forest Mother? What the hell was in that pipe?"

"You smoked it, too. You didn't see her?"

In a voice Charity recognized as a former president, Rene answered, "I didn't inhale."

"How long were we there?"

Rene glanced at his watch. "We were on the ground for less than fifteen minutes."

The conversation she'd had with the shaman and the apparition began to come back to her then. "No," she said, shaking her head. "We were on the ground much longer. It became dark and then light again."

"The old man's got some powerful shit," Rene said, with a chuckle. "Are you sure you're okay to fly?"

Charity looked inside herself, a skill she'd learned from the Bethesda shrinks after returning from Afghanistan five years ago. Her motor skills seemed as sharp as always, her head clear, and her eyesight normal. There was no headache like she'd gotten from smoking weed, trying to tamp down the nightmares. In fact, in all ways, she felt better than she had in a long time. She felt focused. She felt as sharp and on her game as she had seven years earlier, standing on a platform at the start of her best event in the 2000 Olympics.

"Yeah," she replied, putting her aviator sunglasses on. "I can fly just fine. Hang on."

Pushing the cyclic to the right and pulling back slightly, Charity stomped on the right pedal, whipping the Huey around a tight bend in the river. With the skids of the bird nearly skimming the branches on the left side of the river, and the rotors only feet from the water, she felt the familiar weight as g-forces increased in the sharp turn.

Just ahead, a boat raced toward them. Adrenaline began coursing through her brain as she leveled off, slowing time like a slow motion video. She instantly recognized the man at the wheel of the boat. It was the same man who had shot at her yesterday. Napier had said his name was Karl Aleksander.

Next to him was another man, dressed a little better, with an air of authority. He looked trim and handsome, with short blond hair streaming back over his head. For a fraction of a second, their eyes met. She saw evil in his bright blue eyes, and committed his features to memory.

"Vicente said the babo was approaching," Charity said as they roared over the boat. "That's him, next to the driver."

Rene's head turned quickly as the boat flashed past. "Two men in the bow, both armed."

Charity whipped the helo around another bend and into the long straight section beyond it. She pitched the nose downward even more, accelerating to fifty knots. Pressing gently on the left pedal, she turned the Huey slightly sideways, allowing her to see behind them.

"They're gaining!" she shouted, instinctively twisting the throttle to full power and pulling back on the cyclic.

Just as the chopper responded, Charity heard two cracking noises and Rene screamed out, "I'm hit!"

Charity quickly yanked the cyclic left and then right,
climbing up over the jungle canopy on the west side of the
river. She glanced over at Rene, who was leaning forward,
pressing a wadded handkerchief against the top of his
right shoulder.

"Are you all right?" she asked, very concerned.

"Yeah," Rene replied. "Just a nick. What the hell are
those guys shooting at us for?"

"We're interlopers," Charity said, remembering the
words of the apparition. "Like the people of the forest,
those men consider anyone not of their race to be inferior."

Rene looked over at her. "Inferior? What the hell's that
supposed to mean?"

"Those men are descendants of World War Two Nazis."

"And they think we're infer..." Rene began. "Wait, you
told the old man your name was Charity Styleski. Polish?"

"My great-grandfather was a Polish Jew," Charity said.
"Are you sure you're okay?"

"Yeah, I'll be fine. So these guys know you're Jewish?
Don't tell me that's why they were shooting at us."

"No, my grandfather was Jewish, but married a Catholic. Dad was raised a Catholic. I guess I'm agnostic, if that
needs to be clarified. But I know who and what those
people are. The Forest Mother told me all about the things
they've done against the people of the forest."

"The Forest Mother told you, huh?"

Charity considered the question a moment, knowing
that it sounded crazy as hell. But part of her knew that

what she'd experienced was more than just a drug-induced hallucination.

"Sounds nuts, huh? But I don't think I was imagining what I saw and heard. Maybe some kind of out-of-body experience, I don't know."

"That's your real name, then?"

"No, my grandfather dropped the last two letters from his family name when he immigrated to the States to escape the Nazis. My name is Charity Styles."

"It suits you," Rene said. "Are these people your target?"

"Only their leader," Charity replied. "And maybe those three guys on the boat with him."

Flying high over the jungle canopy, she pushed the Huey to its top speed of nearly one hundred and forty miles per hour. At that speed, the settlement was less than ten minutes downriver and the boat would probably take twice that to get there.

"Are you sure you're all right?" Charity asked. "I want to look at something, and we might be there for a few minutes."

"Something those guys back there don't want you to see, I bet. Sure, just don't hang out long enough for them to catch up. I really don't like getting shot."

The way he said it led Charity to believe this wasn't Rene's first time being shot. She looked over at him and, though he was pressing the handkerchief firmly to his shoulder, he didn't appear to be in a great deal of pain and was actively searching the jungle ahead as well as the skies around them.

As they approached the huge clearing, with its massive wall down the center, Rene let out a soft whistle. "Damn, those guys have a serious issue with keeping anything out. Is this their camp?"

Slowing the chopper to almost hovering, Charity turned and flew over the south side of the tall wooden structure, looking for anything. "Yeah, they settled here in the mid-forties. The original inhabitants were all German soldiers who deserted just before the end of the war."

Several men could be seen in the field, none of them holding a weapon any greater than an axe. Three fires were going, and the chopper's downwash whipped the flames to greater intensity.

"They're clearing the underbrush," Rene said. "Burning it."

Two stands on top of the wall, both equidistant from each other and the two rivers were empty. Beyond the wall, a number of women and children came out of the rows of crops to look up as the chopper slowly flew over.

Charity saw all these things in an instant, dismissing everything as non-threatening—all except one man, who was pulling open a large door in the middle of the wall.

"Watch the guy going through the door," Charity said, while examining the wall and the field where the men were working.

"He's climbing up into one of the stands," Rene said. "I think it's time we get the hell outta here."

From the corner of her eye, Charity could see the man reaching the platform. She pulled in maximum power again, pushing the cyclic forward and far to the right. The chopper banked sharply, flying low over the lookout stand and accelerating. Flashing over the crops in the adjacent field, Charity pitched the bird over on its other side, pulling back on the cyclic and then to the right, banking that way in a zig-zag maneuver.

Once over the main part of the settlement, she leveled off, keeping the nose low to gain speed. In just a few seconds, the Huey flew low over the pier at the tip of the island, where the two branches of the Manamo rejoined. In another second, they rose over the jungle canopy again, flying full speed toward Trinidad.

CHAPTER  THIRTY:

Instead of flying to the airport, Charity flew along the east coast of the island, then up into the mountains, landing at Napier's house. She didn't want to risk anyone noticing Rene's bloody shirt, or the bullet holes in the chopper, and asking questions.

As the rotors slowed, Charity unbuckled her harness and went aft. "Come back here; I have a first aid kit."

She slid both doors open to let the breeze in, and instructed Rene to sit on the deck at one of the doors. "Take off your shirt," she told him, as the one-eyed giant and a very small island woman came out of the hangar. The woman was wearing only cut-off jeans, and didn't appear to be modest about it at all. Both of them walked straight toward the chopper.

"What are you doing here?" Napier asked.

His tone and sheer size caused Rene to pull the Kimber from his pocket and point it at the giant. Both Napier and the half-naked woman stopped in their tracks, Napier moving both hands out away from his body.

"He's been shot," Charity replied. "I didn't want to risk any curious questions at the airport."

"Easy, man," Napier said, speaking to Rene. "No need to get all Rambo up in here."

"Rene, meet Thurman. He's the man that guided me upriver yesterday," Charity said, stretching a QuikClot bandage over the wound on Rene's shoulder. "The bullet just grazed you—a little tissue and blood loss, but it'll be fine in a few days." She stepped around Rene and dropped lightly to the ground, helping him to his feet before turning to Napier. Even at five-ten, she had to crane her neck to look up at the man. "You have anything to patch bullet holes? Maybe some black paint?"

"Sure," he replied. "Anything vital hit?" Then he grinned and said, "I mean besides your friend there?"

Rene tucked his pistol back in his pocket and followed Charity to the back of the Huey, both of them examining everything they could see. On the right side, Charity found oil seeping down from the cowling and turned to Napier. "I need a ladder."

"I don't," the big man replied, going down on one knee beside the helicopter, "so I ain't got one. Put your hands against the aircraft and step up onto my shoulders."

With Rene's help, she managed to climb up on the big man's back. Precariously balanced on his shoulders, Charity walked her hands up the side as Napier stood up.

There were two bullet holes in the cowling, invisible from the ground. From a pouch on her belt, Charity took out a Snoopy tool and turned the Dzus locks holding the cowling in place and handed it down to Rene. Using her pen light, she looked closely at the high-pressure oil line that had been repaired at Gitmo. Seeing no seepage there, she checked the rest of the lines.

"Dammit! One of the bullets nicked a low-pressure oil line."

"What size is it?" Thurman asked.

Charity leaned in to look closer at the writing on the rubber hose. "Three-eighths, ID."

"Got some in the hangar, Rambo," Napier said to Rene. "Far side, over the work bench."

The woman had wandered over to the side of the house and returned wearing a bikini top, which didn't really hide much more than she was baring earlier.

"How long?" Rene asked. "And what do you need to remove the damaged one?"

Before Charity could answer, Napier said, "Low pressure hoses only have a tension-clamp. There's a pair of pliers on the workbench."

"About a foot long," Charity said.

The repair only took a couple of minutes, and Thurman even had the right kind of oil on hand to top off the oil reservoir. Once Charity had the cowling back in place, Napier again went down to one knee and she dropped lightly to the ground.

"Thanks," she said to the giant, and turned toward the small woman. "Can you give us a moment?"

Thurman looked at the woman and nodded toward the hangar. "There's a can of black spray paint on the top shelf of the locker beside the workbench, Jade. Just below that is a can of milled fiberglass and resin. Can you bring those to me?"

The woman trotted after Rene, who was already halfway to the hangar, returning the pliers. Once they were out of earshot, Charity said to Napier, "I want to move up the schedule. You have any trouble running me upriver at night?"

"Most nights? No," he replied, scratching his bearded face. "No moon tonight, though."

"I have night-vision optics."

"I don't know," he said.

Charity sensed his reluctance to do it at all. "Come on, big guy," she said, knowing that money wouldn't be the enticement he needed. "It'll be a thrill."

CHAPTER THIRTY-ONE:

"It flew very slowly along the south side of the wall," Erik Wirth told Beisch, when the boat returned an hour after leaving.

The babo turned to Karl. "This is a problem. What do you think they were doing here?"

"Reconnaissance," Karl replied. "I know I hit it. That is not an ordinary helicopter."

Beisch thought for a moment. "Send one man back to the settlement in the boat. Tell him to bring two more men with rifles immediately. Have all your security people but two come here on foot and plan to stay for a while." Then he turned to Wirth, as Karl went back to the boat. "Continue working to clear the field. If the helicopter dropped men off at one of the farms, it will take them at least until sunset to get here. Keeping that field clear allows the *wächters* to see anything or anyone approaching."

Wirth passed the orders to his men, and they filed back through the door to the other side of the wall. Karl and

Rolph returned, as David Hoffman roared off in the boat. Pointing to the furthest lookout platform, Karl said, "Take the other one, Rolph. We will leave the farmer in this one for now." To Beisch he added, "In a few minutes, I will have my men in both stands, and three more in the tree line beyond the wall. They will be able to hear anything approaching the clearing from the jungle."

"Do you think we are in danger?" Wirth asked the babo. "My workers all have guns in their homes, and if there will be trouble, I would like to send the women and children to the settlement."

"There is no danger now," Beisch replied. "Karl is just being overly cautious." Looking up and down the wall, he added, "When it starts to get dark, bring the men back over here and retire for the night. But get that field as clear as possible before then. Karl's men will double up on the watch tonight and the rest of them will camp by the door."

Minutes later, the boat returned with David Kohler and two more of Karl's security team. Karl went through the door with them, pointing and assigning positions. When he returned, he said to the babo, "I will relieve the farmer in this tower. Four of my men will be here in the ATV shortly and the rest should be here in an hour. We will make camp here and the night watchmen will join us at sunset." Wanting to be rid of the babo and take charge personally, he added, "That leaves only two of my team at the settlement. They will be at the main house, awaiting your orders."

"Very good," Beisch replied. "I will return in the boat and send runners out to inform the settlement to be vigilant."

"We will need our radios," Karl said. "Relying on runners to carry messages from the towers to the camp will take too long."

"Does either of the men at the main house know how to operate the boat?"

"Yes, both do," Karl replied, knowing exactly what the babo wanted him to do. "If you will let either man know, he can bring the radios to me in the boat and then return to the main house."

"I am relying on you, Karl."

Beisch then turned to Wirth. "Keep your men working, *Herr* Wirth. Karl has everything under control and will order your men out of the field if there is any trouble."

Karl grinned as the babo turned and went down toward the boat. "Join your men, Wirth. I will make sure nothing happens here."

Erik scowled at the younger man, jabbing a thick finger at his shoulder. "You just keep your eyes open. Leave the real work to real men." Without waiting for a reply, Erik hefted his big, double-bladed axe to his shoulder and disappeared through the door.

Karl looked around for Jenifer and saw her turning into the rows of corn. He trotted quickly after her and called out her name. When she turned, he said, "There is nothing to worry about. I will make sure that no harm comes."

"I know," she replied. "But you do not have to be mean to my father." She stepped through the corn row and disappeared.

Karl went back to the wall, slung his rifle on his shoulder, and called out to the farmer in the tower. "Come down and go help the others. I will take over."

Under the small roof of the lookout platform, Karl had a clear view of the field and the men working. He waved at Rolph in the other tower, getting his attention. He cupped his hands around his mouth and shouted, "The radios will be here soon!"

Looking out over the field, he saw David and the other two security men fanning out toward the jungle, their rifles at the ready.

Hearing engine sounds, Karl turned and saw the boat pulling up on shore. He waved at Rudolph Klein, who climbed out of the boat with a large canvas bag.

"Bring one up here," Karl called down. Though not as good with a rifle as most of his other men, Rudolph was strong and fearless. Perfect for the job of protecting the babo.

When Klein reached the top of the ladder, Karl took the small hand-held radio and pointed across the clearing, explaining where David and the others were. "Take a radio to each of them and one to Rolph in the other tower. Then go back to the main house to protect the babo."

"Right away," Klein said, climbing back down. He shouldered the bag and began trudging toward the other tower.

Karl heard the sound of the ATV approaching. "Wait!" he shouted down. "Help whoever that is in the ATV to unload the gear, then use the machine to deliver the radios."

Klein and the other four men quickly unloaded the supplies. Then Klein roared off on the ATV, leaving the others to begin setting up the camp. Karl watched and checked in with each of his men as the radios were delivered, explaining the situation. Fifteen minutes later, Klein returned, parked the ATV and went back to the boat.

Karl keyed the talk button on the radio and said, "David, this is Karl. You three stay quiet and out of sight over there. Report anything out of the ordinary that you see or hear in the jungle."

"We will," Hoffman replied. "How long will we be out here?"

"A few hours," Karl said. "At dusk, I will call you back here and we will set up double watches in the towers."

Karl watched the tree line and the men working in the field, occasionally shouting down at them, directing the clearing operation. Wirth swung his big axe, taking down small trees with a single blow.

As the sun neared the tops of the jungle canopy to the west, Karl saw the rest of his men coming out of the tree line where the farmers' houses were. Satisfied with the work the men in the field had done, he yelled down, "Wirth, leave three men to tend the fires and the rest can break for supper."

Erik yelled to his workmen, ordering three of them to keep moving debris to the fires and the rest to go home to eat. Shouldering his axe, he went to the door in the wall. There he leaned his axe against the wall and took up the hunting rifle the man who had been in the tower had left.

The last of the debris in the field was tossed onto the fires well before darkness set in. Wirth remained by the door until the men were finished, and then ordered them to go eat. As the sun neared the horizon at the northwest end of the crop field, it lengthened the shadow cast from the wall. The two regular night watchmen arrived, and Karl and Rolph left them to the stands to join the rest of the men at the makeshift camp, where food was being prepared.

"Do you really think that helicopter dropped men off at the farms?" one of the men asked while they all ate around a camp fire.

"I told the babo we should go to the farms and see," Karl replied. "But he thought it too dangerous."

"So we do not know if or how many?" Rolph asked.

"Does not matter. They would have to come through the jungle, cross the field, and then get over the wall. With all twenty of us here, that will never happen."

After eating, Karl assigned a two-hour watch schedule, with two men in each tower and two more on guard at the door at all times. He assigned himself and Rolph the first watch in the towers, but didn't feel any trouble would come for a few hours, if at all.

The two regular *wächters* were fresh, having slept through most of the day, so Karl planned to keep them in the towers throughout the night, which was normal for them. That way, the whole camp wouldn't be alerted by some sound in the jungle that happened ordinarily. In the morning, he would reduce the watch to just one man in each tower.

Just after dark, Wirth came out to the camp. "I do not like the idea of our women and children remaining if trouble is coming."

Karl studied the man's face in the flickering firelight. Half a head taller than Karl, the farmer was big, as big men went. His work had built muscle on muscle and callus on callus, and he probably outweighed Karl by nearly twenty kilos.

"Are you afraid of the dark, old man?" Karl chided.

Erik looked down at him with an icy stare. "There are things out there in the night that you *should* be afraid of.

Only *kinder* fear the darkness. My concern is that one of you *idioten* might shoot in the wrong direction when a tapir comes into the clearing."

"Watch your mouth, old man," Karl said, noticing that several of his men had tensed at the slur, and the others were watching his own reaction. "Go back to your home." Then, turning the man's own words against him, Karl added, "Let the real men protect you."

Wirth looked at the men around the fire, seeing that several were primed for a fight right then and there. "Ha! I can take any three of you *kinder* at once. Stay away from our homes, if you know what is good for you." Turning his back on the men around the fire, Erik stalked off, muttering to himself and shaking his head.

Waiting until Wirth had disappeared through the tall corn, Karl said, "Everyone get some rest. You all know who to awaken when it is time to be relieved."

CHAPTER
THIRTY-TWO:

Charity woke when the alarm on her watch went off. It was an hour before midnight, and she'd had a solid seven hours of sleep after repairing the bullet holes and flying back to the airport. Napier had been reluctant to go in at night, saying that the sound of the big engines would wake the dead.

The big man apparently hadn't read the entire operator's manual, and Charity showed him how to muffle the engines. The black hull would be nearly invisible in the darkness and the only sound while idling would be a slight bow wave from the twin hulls. That little detail had sealed the deal for Napier and he'd promised to meet her at a little used dock south of Port of Spain at midnight.

Rene had been mostly quiet during the short flight and the ride back to the hotel on his scooter. In the elevator, he'd waited until she pressed the button for her floor and had then punched the button for his own.

Charity hadn't been disappointed. The last thing she needed was to spend half the night bouncing around on the bed with the man. It was time to go to work. Before the elevator reached her floor, her mind had moved on to tactical mode. She'd simply said goodbye, and stepped out, walking quickly down the hall to her room, without looking back.

It's for the best, she thought, as she dressed in loose-fitting black cargo pants and a black tank top. Her choice of clothing wouldn't be unusual in a town where tourists partied all night.

She'd stowed anything else she thought she'd need on the boat before leaving Napier's little airfield. She shouldered her bag and took one last look around the room to make sure she hadn't left anything. On the balcony, she was amazed at the number of stars visible, almost like being out on the water.

Outside, Devon was already waiting, parked away from the other cab drivers, but leaning against a friend's cab talking to the driver. He pushed away from the car when Charity approached.

"Heah at eleven, jest like yuh ask, Miss."

"Thanks for being punctual, Devon," Charity replied.

He opened the door of his cab for her and she got in the backseat, as he trotted around to the driver's door. The inside of the cab smelled like marijuana smoke.

"Where to, Miss?" Devon asked, as he drove through the parking lot toward the entrance.

"Do you know the deep water marina in Brickfield?"

The man looked at her in his mirror, frowning. "A dangerous place, more so at night."

"I'm meeting a boat there," Charity replied.

Devon shrugged and turned right, heading for the outskirts of town. "It will take thirty or forty minutes. It is on di other side of Caroni Swamp."

The drive took forty-five minutes, and Charity spent the time reading the target's file again on her tablet. The lack of information on the leader was troubling, but she at least knew what he looked like now.

When the cab came to a stop, Charity looked out. The small parking lot was deserted. A single light pole did very little to illuminate the lot, much less the shadows around the edge of the lot. A few lights on the pier itself revealed not a single boat tied up there.

Where the hell is that one-eyed freak? Charity thought, opening the door and getting out.

"Wait here just a minute, Devon," Charity said, as she looked out over the water. In the distance, she heard a throaty engine start, followed quickly by a second. She handed Devon the fare, with a generous tip. "Thanks, I'll call you again in a day or so to pick me up here."

Looking around nervously, Devon thanked her, put the car in gear, and drove away. Charity waited in the darkness, straining her eyes seaward. She could hear the engines as the boat accelerated, but couldn't see any sign of it.

Her hand gripped the Sig inside her bag as she moved toward the dock, still unsure if the boat she was hearing was Napier or just some commercial fisherman.

The low lights on the pier were mounted on top of the rails, and only illuminated the foot of the pier itself. Once she passed them, she could just make out the bow waves of an approaching twin-hulled boat.

It slowed as it neared the pier, and Charity recognized the shape of the hull and T-top. The boat had no lights on, not even the glow from the gauges. Finally, the hulking shape of the man behind the wheel materialized.

"I was beginning to wonder if you'd chickened out," Charity called out as the boat reached the pier.

"Keep your voice down. This is a place for smugglers and pirates."

You should feel right at home, she thought, reaching out to fend the boat away as Napier reversed the engines.

She stepped quickly aboard, and Napier maneuvered the boat with the throttles, turning it around in a tight turn. Once they were away from the pier, he brought the throttles up and the boat accelerated, planing quickly.

"Smugglers and pirates?"

"Yeah," Thurman grunted. "Drug runners and slavers mostly, but anything that's not legal usually comes in or leaves here."

He pushed the throttles more, and the boat increased speed, turning southwest and leaving the dimly lit smuggler's cove behind.

Charity thought it a little ironic that Napier was wearing the night vision headset with two eye-pieces, but a single lens. Leaning over, she opened the small compartment in the side of the console. Feeling around inside, she found the case containing the other set, turned it on, and pulled it over her face.

The night vision optics in the headset gathered available light and intensified it. While she could see clearly in the dark, everything appeared gray-green, depth perception was limited, and peripheral vision was lost beyond the forty-degree capability of the system. The one Charity wore had an added feature, only recently developed in England: she could change from night optics to thermal imaging with the flip of a switch.

The sea was calm, and the light from the stars would be enough to see by, once their eyesight adjusted. But this close to the river delta, any number of things might be floating on the surface. Hitting a log while going fifty knots would spell disaster.

"We'll run dark until we're out of sight from shore," Napier said. "Then we can turn on the spots on the leading edge of the tower. Won't be anyone out here to see us. It's half an hour to the mouth of the river, then almost two more to the settlement."

Charity hoisted herself up onto the seat, while Thurman chose to remain standing at the helm, the leaning post cushion flipped forward on his side. She could easily see over the low, dark-tinted windshield. Occasionally, a startled fish would leap out of the water in front of them, but other than that there was nothing to look at ahead but open sea.

"Remember that big dead tree in the water, about a mile south of the settlement?"

"That where you plan to go in at?" Thurman asked.

"Seemed like the only option."

"You'll still have to get across that field, and they have people watching it. Then there's that big-ass wall."

"The field won't be a problem, but the wall may be a little trickier. Why does Stockwell call you Napper?"

He glanced over at her for a moment, the single lens sticking out of the middle of his face. "Rhymes with Napier."

"Come on," Charity said. "I was in the Army, too. I know nicknames aren't just based on spelling."

"That where you learned to fly that chopper?"

"I was flying a crop-dusting helo long before that," she replied.

He grunted a sort of laugh. "That'd explain the maneuvers."

"Your nickname?" she prodded.

"I served under Colonel Stockwell when he was a young first lieutenant," Thurman said. "Toward the end of the war in Vietnam. You ever hear of sappers?"

"Suicide bombers?"

"Yeah, pretty much the same. Only sappers would charge the wire and blow themselves up when they got tangled in it, breaching the wire for their VC buddies to get through. We were on a two-day patrol, outside the wire. During the night, I was hunkered down in a foxhole with two other guys, when we heard someone running toward us. It was a sapper with a satchel charge strapped to his chest. He came straight at my position and just as he made to dive into the foxhole, I stood up and caught him. Body slammed him so hard it broke his neck. Didn't kill him right off, though. But he couldn't move his hands to pull the detonator and explode the vest. Cat started screaming at us and cussing us in English. Little fucker had a pretty good vocabulary."

"What'd you do?"

"I don't really remember saying anything, but the guys I was with told the rest of the company that I yelled at the VC to shut up and take a nap, just before I crushed the side of his head with my fist."

Charity couldn't help but shudder a little, visualizing a nearly seven-foot tall giant lifting a small Vietnamese soldier and slamming him down, then crushing his skull with a single blow.

"My buddies took to calling me Sapper Napper after that, and it just got shortened to Napper."

"How long were you in the Army?"

"Three years," he replied. "Nixon started drawing down the size of the military, and when I got back from Nam I was discharged. You?"

"Two years. I was a medivac pilot in Afghanistan at the beginning of the current war. Medically discharged."

"And you were a crop duster before that?"

Charity was glad he hadn't dwelt on the subject of her discharge. "No," she replied. "That was before college. Just before the Army, during my college years, I was an Olympic swimmer."

"Get outta here!"

"Yeah. Bronze medalist in the four hundred individual medley at the 2000 games in Sydney."

Though she couldn't see his eye behind the goggles, Napier looked surprised. He turned and studied the side of her face, then moved his gaze down the length of her body. "Your name's not Gabriella Fleming, then," he said.

"Oh?"

"Charity Styles was the bronze medalist in that event in 2000."

It was Charity's turn to be surprised. "You follow the games that close?" she asked.

He chuckled softly. "Just the swimming and diving events. All those little girls tumbling and bouncing around, and all them runners and such, never interested me much."

"You're an odd man, Napper. Yes, that's my real name."

"You should talk," he said, steering the boat around a floating log. "Why'd you give it up?"

"Nine-eleven," she replied.

They rode in silence for a few minutes. Then Napier reached down and flipped a switch on the dash. The water ahead turned blindingly white from the bright spotlights. They both removed the night vision headsets and turned them off to conserve battery power.

"We'll keep the lights on until we're halfway upriver to the settlement," Thurman said, switching on the gauge lights, chart plotter, and radar. The radar screen showed the outline of the coast ahead, but nothing else within its twelve-mile range, so Napier switched it back off.

The spots on the front of the T-top reached out nearly half a mile, illuminating the water ahead of the boat, one light angled slightly higher than the other.

Charity studied the chart plotter, then looked out to the east and west. The plotter showed they were already in the mouth of the delta, but she couldn't see the shoreline on either side. Checking the scale at the bottom, she figured they were in the center of the mile-and-a-half wide delta.

"That's Isla Cotorra to the west," Napier said. "You can just make out the light on the west side just above the trees."

"People live there?"

"No, the light's unmanned. But, there's a little fishing village just ahead, called Capure."

Napier hugged the west bank of *Caño Capure*, a smaller distributary of the Manamo, as they passed the small village. There were no boats on the water and no lights from the village.

Beyond it, the river narrowed and the boat was engulfed by the jungle on both sides. Soon they came out from under the overhanging canopy into the much wider main distributary of the mighty Orinoco, the Manamo River. Here, Napier brought the boat up to thirty knots, following the narrow beam of the spotlights as they continued upriver.

An hour later, they passed what looked like another village, with several thatch huts on stilts. It was at the confluence of a river that joined the Manamo.

"What's that?" Charity asked, pointing.

"*Campamento Boca de Tigre*," Napier replied, picking his night vision headset up from the console. "From here, we go dark and silent the rest of the way."

"Camp Tiger's Mouth?" Charity asked, as she donned her own headset.

Napier switched off the lights, and Charity turned on her optics. The scenery changed to the depthless gray-green once again.

"Jaguar," he replied, as he slowed the boat and engaged the mufflers. The boat couldn't go nearly as fast, muffled. "Some locals still call it *el tigre*, but there ain't no tigers in South America."

Three times over the next hour, Napier had to quickly maneuver the boat around obstacles, two being sandbars and the third a huge crocodile stretched nearly the width of a narrow part of the river in a very shallow spot.

"When you get off the boat," Napier warned, "move as quickly inland as you can. Crocs will be all along the shoreline. Jaguars usually shy away from the scent of a human, but crocs just don't give a shit—and both are night hunters."

"How much further to the settlement?"

"Less than a mile," Napier replied, slowing the boat to just five knots. The gentle swish of the two bows cutting the water was the only sound. "Just around the next bend."

CHAPTER THIRTY-THREE:

Stockwell sat at a large outdoor table on a tiny island in the Keys. The island, situated in the back country just north of Big Pine Key, was owned by Jesse McDermitt. The two had been discussing a pending mission the transporter was involved in. It was dark, still several hours before dawn. McDermitt's island home was remote, but not completely devoid of all things civilized.

"This is damned good coffee, Jesse," Stockwell said, while the retired Marine sniper checked and rechecked his dive gear.

"Rusty, down in Marathon, gets it for me. Comes from a tiny farm in Costa Rica called Hacienda La Minita."

The two drank coffee and discussed the mission, then McDermitt steered the conversation toward Charity and what she was doing. They hadn't discussed it since leaving for Key West two days earlier.

"She's damaged goods," McDermitt finally said, with a great deal of conviction. "She might do well at not showing it, but she could have some sort of flashback to her time in the hands of the Taliban."

Stockwell knew all about what had happened to Charity. Captured, tortured, and raped by the enemy, she'd undergone a whole slew of psychological evaluations when she returned. Though she was found unfit for Army flight status, she was more than qualified for her current assignment. The fact that she could unleash the demons that dwelled in her subconscious, at will, was actually a plus in the eyes of the secretary. But Travis would never repeat that to anyone.

"Everyone on the team undergoes a lot of psychological testing, Jesse. Charity went through even more after I submitted her name to the secretary. All the shrinks say she's okay in the head. Maybe not perfect, but well enough for the duties she was chosen for."

"How does she get around from target to target?" the man asked, as he began checking his M-40 sniper rifle.

Stockwell studied McDermitt over the rim of his mug. He hadn't known him personally for very long, but had read over his bio completely and knew enough to be sure he could be trusted.

Finally, he set his mug down and said, "Only three others have that information: Deuce, the secretary, and the president. I know you well enough to know you can be trusted with it. She's on a forty-five-foot Alden sloop, equipped with the latest nav and comm equipment and anything else she might need for a mission. I'm the only one that has contact with her. I fly to where she is and deliver a target assignment and any specialized gear she'll need. She can choose to decline any target she wants, but so far she's three for three, without a single hiccup."

The last part was a bit of an embellishment. Charity's current mission was only her second and the first hadn't quite gone as planned. In fact, she'd been stood down for a couple of months, while the secretary and the president considered what had happened in Mexico.

McDermitt arched an eyebrow. "An Alden sloop?"

"Her own choice," Stockwell replied. "She only agreed to take the assignment if that's how she would travel. It was originally built eighty years ago, but underwent a two-month refit, sparing no cost. Her assignment area is the whole Caribbean Basin, so she can usually get to where she needs to in less than a week. During that time, she makes her own plan as to when, where, and how to eliminate the target."

"Did the shrinks take into account that she'd be alone at sea?" McDermitt pressed. "Just her and her thoughts?"

Just then, the door to the makeshift communications building opened and Stockwell heard the heavy thump-thump of an inbound helicopter. Two men came out of the building and split up, heading to the four corners of the large clearing, where they placed strobes on the ground and activated them. Both men were wearing black wetsuits and jump boots.

McDermitt began pulling on his own wetsuit. "I don't like it, Travis. Not even a little bit. Probably because I know her better than most. While she and I were on the *Revenge* last year, she opened up to me. Took her a week, but she finally talked about what happened to her in Afghanistan and how devastated she was when Jared was killed."

A year ago, Charity had been involved with a young man who'd been dishonorably discharged from the

Marine Corps under bogus conditions. McDermitt had been instrumental in getting the discharge overturned, allowing him to reenlist. The man responsible for the bad paper, and ultimately for Jared's death, was none other than Stockwell's predecessor, Jason Smith. He'd once been a CIA operative during the early stages of the war. McDermitt and Charity had spent more than two weeks aboard his charter boat, hunting the man down as he moved around the Caribbean.

"But she took care of the problem then," Travis said. "Just as she's doing now."

"You weren't there, Colonel. You didn't see the look in her eyes when she did it."

CHAPTER THIRTY-FOUR:

apier hugged the bank of the river, as far from the settlement as possible, as they silently approached. The boat from which the men had shot at her chopper was tied off to the pier at the northern tip of the island. The river split there, and Napier took the eastern main channel. A large structure not far from the pier had a light in a single window on the ground floor. Through the night optics, the light illuminated half an acre of manicured lawn as well as several adjacent buildings. Other than that, the small village was completely dark.

The black boat melted into the dark jungle, invisible to anyone on shore. The engines were so quiet that, had she not known they were moving against the current, Charity would have thought the boat was drifting with it. Napier guided the boat upriver, barely moving. Soon the main body of the settlement was behind them, and a dim glow could be seen ahead, just around a bend in the river.

Charity leaned close to Napier. "What's that light coming from?" she softly whispered.

Napier didn't answer for a moment as they neared the bend. The light wasn't steady, but rose and fell in intensity. Charity lifted her headset and saw absolutely nothing. No light, no river, no bank, not even the bow of the boat. Nothing.

"Camp fire," the big man beside her quietly whispered. "Near the wall."

As they approached the bend, the wall came into view, glowing softly from the light of a small fire. Charity switched to thermal optics as they rounded the bend. The fire itself looked like a white hot-spot, and the wall near it glowed slightly from the heat of the fire.

The first tower was above the wall and closer to the river. She easily made out two figures in the tower. As the boat moved slowly forward, more hot spots appeared. More than a dozen were arranged around the fire in horizontal positions. Two more appeared to be men standing away from the fire, and two more could be seen in the far tower. She switched back to night optics, revealing the two men standing by the door in the wall, with tents scattered around the fire. None seemed to see or hear the quiet, black boat as it slipped past. But Napier had his hand on the throttles, ready to jam them to the stops if anyone did.

"They know you're coming," Napier whispered, watching the tower and the men by the door closely.

"They think *someone* is coming," she quietly replied. *But they won't be ready when I do*, she thought.

Moving slowly past the wall, Charity looked across the field beyond it. The high brush had been mostly cleared. She switched back to thermal and saw three warm glows in the middle of the field, spread apart by several hundred feet. She scanned the field all around, but saw no other heat signatures.

Switching back to night vision, she quickly pinpointed where the warm spots were. *They'd cleared and burned the brush.*

Minutes later, well away from the wall and the men beyond it, Napier nudged the throttles slightly and the boat increased speed.

"I think you should abort," he said quietly.

"Don't worry about me," Charity said. "Just get me to shore up here and I'll get past them somehow."

"You're fucking nuts, lady. You know that?"

That's the point, she thought.

"Just get me ashore," she repeated, "and this will all be over before the sun comes up."

"I still think you're nuts," Napier said, as he guided the boat around another turn in the river, the large tree they'd seen two days earlier looming in the distance.

Charity went forward and began to gather her equipment. Getting from the boat to the tree, and then to the ground with all her gear, would be the hard part. She put on her black tactical jacket first, then slung her rifle over her head and right shoulder, allowing it to rest easily across her chest. Adjusting the sling so that the rifle clung closely between her breasts, she pulled on her backpack and moved to the bow.

Napier guided the boat in close to the up-current side of the massive tree trunk, allowing the current to drift it back against the huge fallen tree. He brought the boat to a stop just past where the upper part of the tree disappeared into the dark water, and quickly looped a line around a broken branch and tied off. Leaving the engines running in neutral, he moved past Charity and tied the bow line off to another branch.

"I won't be far away," he whispered. "I'll continue upriver to Tucupita, just past the farms." He opened a small hatch in the starboard side of the console and reached inside. "Here," he said, handing her a small VHF radio and ear plug. "This has a scanner function, and I have another just like it. If you get into any trouble, call me on any frequency and I should be able to hear you. The village is only ten miles further upriver, and I can be back here in fifteen minutes."

Charity stuck the radio into a cargo pocket and turned to the giant man. "Thanks, Napper."

She turned and struggled up onto the gunwale, before Napier grabbed her around her slim waist and easily lifted her up to straddle the giant tree trunk.

"Be careful, Charity Styles," Napier said. "I'd sure like to see you swim again one day. You were a gold medalist in my book."

Before she could reply to the man's goofy comment, he loosened the bow line and shoved the boat away from the tree, then quickly moved to the stern, untying that line and guiding the boat toward the middle of the river again.

The tree she was on was massive, old-growth timber, so large her legs didn't even reach halfway around the trunk. The bark was rough and not yet beginning to rot. Charity figured it had probably fallen within the last six months, maybe during the last flood.

Switching to thermal, she looked ahead toward the base of the great tree to make sure it wasn't hiding a predator. Seeing nothing, she switched back to night vision. The trunk was wide enough that she could easily walk up it, using protruding branches for hand holds.

She rose slowly, gripping a large branch that stuck out at an angle next to her. It was slow going, but she was finally able to get past the tangle of branches above the brush at the water's edge, to the massive root system of the tree. There, she was nearly fifteen feet off the ground. She looked back toward the water and saw Napier about a hundred yards upriver, the boat unmoving against the current, as he watched her. She waved and saw him wave back, then slowly began climbing down the huge roots of the tree.

Dropping to the ground from five feet, she crouched, drew her Sig, and looked all around. Switching to thermal, she scanned the area again, remembering what Napier had said about crocodiles and jaguars. Seeing nothing, she switched back to night vision and started inland.

Suddenly, just ahead of her, what appeared to be a fallen tree trunk moved, twisting toward her. In an instant, she realized that crocodiles were cold-blooded and wouldn't give off a heat signature. *Big mistake*, she thought and cursed herself as she danced around the beast's tail and ran headlong into the dense jungle beyond it.

Safely away, breathing heavily through her mouth, Charity stopped and looked back. No movement and no sound. Checking her compass, she turned and started moving quietly through the jungle toward the wall, figuring it would take thirty minutes to reach it.

Still fifty yards from the clearing, she could clearly see the two towers, illuminated by the small fire on the other side. Thermal imaging showed two men still in each tower. The light of the fire would reduce the capability of their night vision optics, if they had any. It was very doubtful they had thermal imaging, since the technology was only recently made available in a size small enough to be man-portable.

Crouching low anyway, Charity moved slowly toward the edge of the clearing, where she squatted down beside a large log and removed her pack and rifle.

The four men in the towers posed little threat. Quietly, she removed the suppressor from a long pocket on the side of the pack and threaded it onto the rifle's barrel. At this distance, she could easily kill both men in one tower before they could raise an alarm, and then do the same with the other two.

Stockwell's words about what had happened at the volcano in Mexico echoed in Charity's mind. Though she'd been sent in to kill one man, she'd killed nearly everyone in the terrorist camp. He'd told her that the secretary was ready to pull the plug on her assignment if anything like that happened again. From another pouch in the pack, she removed the suppressor for the Sig and threaded it on, just in case.

This was a little different, though. In Mexico, the terrorist leader had been the first to fall, and then she'd gone into a bloodlust frenzy. Now she had twenty armed men between her and her intended target. She doubted he would be the type to join these men at their camp. Most likely, he was holed up in the big house by the pier where she'd seen the light.

She studied the wall, zooming the optics to full power. It extended a good fifteen feet out into the piranha- and crocodile-infested water. No way to swim around it.

There, she thought. *Near the end.* The top of the wall stepped down as it moved out into deeper water, each board a few inches shorter than the previous one. But for some reason, the last board was maybe two inches higher than the one before it.

Digging into her pack, Charity pulled out the package Stockwell had sent to the hotel and opened it. Inside was a ghillie suit like the ones worn by snipers in the field, along with two rolls of cloth material laced with tattered thread.

She heard the old shaman's words in her head: *Move slowly.*

While she kept an eye on the four men in the towers, she scanned the open field between her position and the end of the wall, a plan formulating in her mind. She began selecting weeds, grasses, and large leaves, similar to what was in the field and carefully threaded them into the fabric of the ghillie suit, adding to its camouflage. Satisfied, she took the two rolls and carefully wrapped the fabric around her rifle, starting at the suppressor.

Nearly ready, she heard a low voice from across the field. In the nearest tower, one of the men had disappeared. She looked at the other tower and the head of one of the two there ducked below the wall. A minute later the man in the first tower reappeared.

No, she thought, looking closer. *Not the same man.* Another voice drifted across the clearing and a few minutes later a new man appeared in the further tower.

Watch relief, she told herself. *But why change only one man?*

She waited a few minutes, watching both of the small towers closely as the new men got comfortable in the cramped spaces. Then it came to her. The towers were usually manned by only one sentry each. Men whose regular job it was to stay up there all night. The men around the fire and the added lookouts were reinforcements, unaccustomed to pulling an all-nighter.

They were definitely expecting an attack or something. Maybe someone had heard her helicopter, even though she'd swung far to the east, away from the settlement, before arriving at Vicente's farm. If they'd heard her and sent the men in the boat to investigate, they might have thought an attack force had been dropped off.

Calculating the distance in her head and judging by the density of the jungle she'd just come through, she doubted a group of men could make it from Vicente's farm to here in much less than a day, and the men in the camp would surely know that. It'd only been about eighteen hours. An overabundance of caution?

She quietly struggled into the ghillie suit, after first removing the things she thought she'd need from her pack and attaching them to her belt under the ghillie top.

When she was prepared, Charity quietly slipped over the log and went down into a prone position, her rifle beneath her. McDermitt had taught all of her former team the proper way to move using the suit. Deliberately, she pushed the rifle forward, inch by inch. Slower still, she crept forward and covered it. The ghillie top had a hood that completely covered her face. It had two small holes for the headset lenses to stick out of and a mesh opening at her mouth to breathe through.

Over the next hour, she stealthily made her way across the clearing, angling toward the spot where the wall reached the river. It didn't take long before it became very hot and uncomfortable inside the suit. She'd been warned about this, and though it was still spring back in the States, she was only a few degrees north of the equator here and knew she'd have to stay hydrated.

Halfway across the clearing, she stopped to take a break. Slowly bringing the tube from the canvas water bladder on her back up to her mouth, she drank while watching the towers and listening. The two men in the nearer tower, now only a couple of hundred feet off to her left, were talking quietly, only one of them really looking out over the field.

At his distance, she could tell that neither of these two men had any kind of night vision optics, and they were relying solely on the light from the stars. The night sky was clear and, even though there wasn't a moon, she knew that as long as they didn't look toward the fire, their eyes would adjust to the darkness.

Ever so slowly, she began pushing the rifle ahead again and pulling herself up over it. To this point, she'd moved only four or five feet per minute. Closer now, she knew she'd have to go even slower.

The whole concept of the ghillie suit was to be nearly invisible against a background that looked like the suit. But, fast movement couldn't be hidden. The surrounding grass was a foot tall, which helped as she crept forward again, slowly parting the grass and filling it with her body.

Finally, at the base of the wall, she looked at her watch. It had taken over two hours to get across the field and the sun would be coming up in less than two more hours. A tiny slice of the moon would rise just before the sun, probably in less than an hour.

Charity reached under her and unhooked from her belt a small grappling hook attached to thirty feet of lightweight line. She was just about ready to rise to a kneeling position, when she heard a large splash off to her right and froze.

Ever so slowly, she turned her head toward the near tower. Both men were leaning out and looking in her direction. There was another splash, a little further away and both men laughed, retreating back inside the tower. When she looked out over the river, she saw a huge crocodile swimming away with some hapless creature in its mouth. Scanning the shoreline, she spotted another croc, partly out of the water in the shallows, not twenty feet away, waiting patiently for his next meal.

There was a small bush to her right, apparently overlooked by the men clearing the field. She slowly made her way to the other side of the bush and rose to a crouch, slinging her rifle over her head and shoulder again. Reaching under her shirt, she opened a flap on one of the many pouches on her belt and removed a heavy steel shot about a half inch in diameter. With her left hand, she pulled her slingshot from its pouch.

Charity wasn't too concerned about the men in the far tower. They were much too far away to see or hear what she was about to do. The men in the near tower were her only concern. Slowly, she shook out the grappling line and got ready. She'd have only one chance; if she missed the spot at the top of the wall with the high end board, the hook would splash into the water. No telling what kind of debris was down there on the bottom and the grapple might get snagged on something.

When she was ready, she aimed the slingshot up toward the top of the wall, angling to the left so the shot would land directly behind the men in the tower. She released it and waited. After a couple of seconds, there was a loud thunk as the shot hit something solid on the other side of the wall.

Not waiting to see if the men in the tower took the bait, she stood and swung the hook two times, before releasing it. Dropping back to a crouch, she watched the grapple fall across the second board from the end, just where she wanted it. There was a dull thud as it fell against the wood. Taking up the slack, she tugged, making sure the hook was set, then turned and looked up at the tower about a hundred yards away.

The two men were leaning away from the wall, looking out over the camp. Knowing that their night vision was now ruined by the low firelight, she stood and ran toward the spot where the croc lay in the shallows, taking up the line as she went.

At the water's edge, she leapt up and grabbed the line as high as possible, lifting her legs out ahead of her. The crocodile, splashed and lunged at her, but moved too slowly, as she sailed out of its reach. As she reached the bottom of the arc, she felt the hook slide along the top of the wall and catch on the slightly higher last board.

There was a shout from the tower, but it was too late to do anything now. Charity reached the apex of the arcing swing and she kicked her body around, hoping there wasn't another crocodile lying in wait on the other side of the wall. At the last moment, she loosened her grip and slid to the ground on the other side of the wall, still holding the line.

Dropping quickly to a crouch, she drew her Sig and prepared to shoot anything that moved, man or beast. Nothing moved. She'd landed in a slight depression, probably created by the river's water moving around the wall during the flood. Craning her neck, she looked over the natural berm at the camp, just in time to see the men in the tower turn back to the side she'd just left, one of them shining a powerful flashlight toward the water. Both men laughed nervously and called down to the two men at the door in German.

Charity spoke some German, though they were too far away to make out anything for certain. She did hear the word *krokodil* and thanked the big reptile for helping with her diversion.

The line was looped around the end of the wall. She flipped it in a loop out over the last board and the grapple fell. She jerked the line quickly, and the grapple fell into the mud at the river's edge. Charity hauled it in, coiled the line and reattached it to her belt.

The crops were only twenty feet away, and Charity slowly crawled toward the first row, then disappeared into the maze of vegetables.

CHAPTER THIRTY-FIVE:

Erik Wirth woke with a start, a loud thud disturbing his restless slumber. He heard something bounce and roll off the roof of the house. Getting quickly to his feet, he went to the closet and grabbed his hunting rifle.

"What is it, Karl?" his wife asked. Gretchen was a stout woman who'd borne him three sons and a daughter. Their three sons had left the settlement a year ago—bent on making it to anywhere else—and they hadn't heard from them since.

"Perhaps nothing," he replied. "Maybe the *wächters* playing tricks. Stay here."

Erik knew she wouldn't. It just wasn't in her nature to be the demure housewife. When he left the bedroom, he heard the bedsprings creak as she got out of bed.

Jenifer's door opened and she stuck her head out. "What was that noise, *Vater*?"

"Probably nothing," he repeated to his only daughter. She'd been acting strangely all afternoon and evening, and hadn't eaten much of anything at dinner. Now there was a look of terror on her usually calm face.

Gretchen came out of the bedroom next to him. "Go to Jenifer," he told his wife, as he moved noiselessly toward the front door, facing the fields.

Opening the door slowly, Erik stepped out onto the porch. It took only a moment for his eyes to adjust to the moonless night, and he stood on the elevated porch and looked out over the small clearing between his home and the crops.

Nothing moved. He heard one of the men out by the wall say something, and several laughed. Quietly, he moved to a rocking chair by the door and sat down. The chair squeaked slightly, protesting his considerable weight.

Out of the corner of his eye, he thought he saw movement. But when he looked in the direction of the first row of corn he saw nothing there.

Erik watched for several minutes, but nothing happened and he didn't hear any more sounds. Through the front door, which was slightly ajar, he could barely hear his wife and daughter whispering to one another. He continued to wait, certain that one of the men out there had thrown a rock onto his roof.

After nearly half an hour, he heard his daughter quietly sobbing, and his wife making comforting sounds. It wasn't like Jenifer to cry over a sound in the night. He rose and, after looking around the yard again, went back inside to check on his wife and daughter.

CHAPTER THIRTY-SIX:

Charity moved quickly through the low rows of what she recognized as tomato plants, some of them blooming. Halfway down the row, she cut to the west, passing rows of other vegetables until she reached the unmistakable corn rows. Ducking through the first row of corn, she turned north, heading toward the small houses tucked under the edge of the jungle canopy.

Just as she reached the end of the row, she heard something creak and froze in her tracks. Slowly, she went down to one knee and looked out across the small clearing between the crops and the houses. A man sat in a rocking chair on the porch of one of the houses. At this range, she could eliminate him easily and continue on. But Stockwell's warning about collateral damage came back to her mind, so she went down into a prone position and stealthily crawled across the yard, angling away from the man on the porch.

A light appeared in the back of the man's house. He didn't seem to notice it, as he stared out over the crops to where the men were camped. As she got abreast of the man's porch, she saw that he was armed, and slowly drew her Sig. At only thirty feet, it would be an easy shot, and she knew she could kill him with just a single round.

Just as she was bringing the gun up, the man stood and went back inside the house. Charity rose and trotted quickly to the corner of the house, then moved slowly toward the rear, where the lighted window was.

Approaching the open window, she heard a girl's quiet sobs and a woman's gentle voice, speaking soothingly in German. "Quiet now, dear. We cannot tell your father. He will surely kill the man."

"Tell me what?" a man's voice said, in an even tone.

There was a rustling sound, and Charity heard heavy footsteps on the wooden floor. In hushed whispers, the woman tried to tell the man that it was nothing.

Then Charity heard a young girl's voice. Through her sobbing and Charity's less than perfect grasp of the German language, she couldn't quite make out what the girl was saying, but could tell she was probably a teenage girl.

The man pressed the issue, and Charity slowly rose to eye level with the window, raising the night vision headset and hood, so she could see inside. The room was dimly lit by a single lantern on a desk just below the window. The man was huge. Not as big as Napier, but nearly as tall as Jesse McDermitt, and much broader in the shoulders and chest.

A woman sat on the edge of a small bed, a pretty blond girl beside her. It was obvious the man was the girl's father; they shared the same hair color, eyes, and facial features. The woman had darker hair, streaked with gray.

Through the girl's sobs, Charity heard her say in German, "Karl took me. I told him no, that we had to wait, but he forced himself on me." Then the girl collapsed against her mother's ample bosom, sobbing.

The woman looked quickly at the man, tears running down her face, as she reached out to him. "No, Erik."

The look on the man's face slowly changed. Charity recognized the rage that lay just beneath the surface, as a single tear streaked down his tan cheek. Without a word, he turned and started back through the door.

Charity knew what she had to do. She knew the girl's father would charge into the camp, looking for the one who had defiled his daughter. She also knew that he would probably get himself killed, and she didn't need the armed men put on edge.

Moving quickly, Charity got to the porch and swung up onto it, as quietly as possible. She had just reached the door when it swung open and the man stepped out. The sound of her Sig's hammer being thumbed back stopped the man halfway across the porch.

"Do not move," she said in German, her words slow and deliberate. "Very slowly and quietly, bend over and lay your rifle on the floor."

"Who are you?" the man said, his voice cracking.

"I am a friend," Charity replied. "But I will kill you if you take another step. Those men out there will kill you if I let you do what you are planning to do."

The man's voice was full of conviction when he said, "I will kill them all with my bare hands."

"I have no doubt that you can in a fair fight," she whispered. "But it is one against twenty and they have guns, too. You will die."

The man's big shoulders drooped and he slowly bent over, laying his rifle on the deck. As he rose, he turned to face Charity and gasped.

She realized what a sight she must be, like a plant come to life. With her Sig leveled at the man, she slowly reached up and slid the hood all the way back, letting the headset fall inside it.

"Who are you?" the man asked again. "Why are you here?"

"I am a friend of the forest people," she replied, searching for the right words in German. "I have come to free them of the babo and his men."

"I speak your language," the man said in broken Spanish. "English as well. How did you get here?"

"I am an American," Charity replied in English.

"American? But why? How did you get here? Did you come in the black helicopter?"

The man's English was better than his Spanish. *Not your average farmer*, Charity thought.

"I flew the helicopter," she replied, now remembering having seen the big man as she flew over. "I was listening at your window just now. I can't let you go out there after the man who raped your daughter. Not yet, anyway. When the time is right, I will let you have your revenge."

Charity heard footsteps coming toward the door and stepped back against the wall, out of sight from inside.

"Erik," the man's wife said in German, "please do not do what you feel you must."

Erik looked inside his house and held a hand up, palm out, stopping his wife. "Stay inside, Gretchen. We have a visitor."

Using the barrel of the Sig, Charity motioned Erik toward the door. Once he was through it, she followed. The woman gasped, clutching a hand to her mouth.

"I will not harm you," Charity said in halting German.

"My wife and daughter both speak English," Erik said, turning to face Charity. "How many are you?"

"I'm here alone," Charity replied. Then taking a chance that the man she was after wasn't well-liked by those under his rule, she added, "I've come to kill the babo."

"Beisch?" Gretchen asked, the tone of her voice telling Charity all she needed to know, as well as the man's name.

"Yes," she replied. "And any of his men that get in my way."

"Not Karl Aleksander," Erik said firmly. "I will kill him with my own two hands for what he has done. But you are one woman and they are many."

Karl Aleksander, Charity thought. The man who shot at her twice. The man responsible for terrorizing Vicente's people and killing many of them.

"They seem to be expecting an army," Charity said. "I had little trouble slipping past them. Will you help me?"

"Yes," his wife replied, before Erik could utter a word. "He has been responsible for many disappearances here and has ordered the murder of many of the people to the south. I think he killed my boys, for wanting only to leave."

The young girl came into the room and was about to scream when Charity turned toward her. Erik held a finger to his lips and said, "This woman is here to help."

The girl wasn't a girl at all. She had the face of one, perhaps in her late teens, but she was already a full-grown woman. Her eyes were red and puffy from crying. She'd changed from her nightgown to jeans and a flannel shirt.

Charity turned toward Erik, not wanting to dwell on the girl. What she'd just gone through brought memories flooding back. Squashing them down, she asked, "How many people are here in the settlement?"

"Here at the farm, or on the whole island?"

"Both."

"Fifty-one here at the farm. Nine families and three single men." He furrowed his brow in thought. "Perhaps seven hundred up the hill in town, nearly all born here. Maybe fifty or sixty have been brought in from outside. We tend to keep to ourselves here on the farm, and it is rare that anyone from town visits."

"How many would you guess would move to protect Beisch?"

"All those out by the wall," Erik replied, pointing with his chin. "None of us at the farm, and only a handful of the townspeople. He is an evil man, worse than his father."

"Are those men out there all the security people?" Charity asked, a plan formulating in her mind.

"Yes," said Erik.

"No," the young girl said, stepping forward. "I over-heard Karl order one man back to the main house where another was already there, to protect Mister Beisch."

Charity holstered the Sig and looked outside. "So those men out there are the only security for the island."

"Beisch's henchmen," Erik corrected her. "Just as black-hearted as him. All of us here at the farm have guns to hunt with. We supply the whole island with food.

Except for what the fishermen in town provide. But we have very little ammunition. Just before a hunt, cartridges are distributed by Aleksander, and any that are unspent are confiscated."

Charity stepped outside and picked up the rifle, recognizing it as an American made bolt-action Winchester with a small scope mounted on it. She carried the rifle back inside and extended it to the big farmer.

"Will you help me?" Charity asked. "I need to get to Beisch's house without any of those men knowing. And I need you to not do anything while I'm gone."

"The sun will be up before you can get there," Erik said. "And it will be impossible for you to get through town without being noticed."

"You said nine families are out here?" Charity asked. "And three single men? So, only twelve men? How many are armed?"

Erik grinned. "We have twenty-five men here at the farm. It would have been twenty-eight with my sons. And all have guns, but no more than a couple of cartridges per man that we have been able to hold back from the hunts."

Charity nodded her head toward the door. "Can I speak to you outside, Erik?"

The big man turned toward his wife and daughter with a serious expression. "Do you have any feelings for this man at all, Jenifer?"

To her credit, the young girl straightened and looked her father in the eye. "I thought I did. I was fooled. He is a monster, no different than Beisch."

"Go to your room," he ordered her. "Stay with her, Gretchen." His wife was about to protest, but Erik cut her off with a single word. "Now."

As they stepped out onto the porch, Charity pulled on the night vision headset, switching it to thermal imaging. She looked all around, noting only a few small heat signatures moving through the corn.

"You have mice in your corn," she told him, removing the headset.

"What is that thing?" Erik asked.

"It allows me to see in the darkness and to see heat from living animals. It's how I was able to sneak past you, as you sat on the porch." She started down the steps, to put a little more distance between them and Erik's family. "There isn't anyone around," she whispered. "I need that vehicle out there and somebody to drive me to where Beisch is."

"What do you propose?" the big man asked.

"You and the other men here?" she began. "You're hunters. Are all the men good with a rifle?"

"The best," he replied. "But Aleksander's men have much more firepower. We can barely put a cartridge in each rifle."

"I can help by giving you the element of surprise. And stealth."

"Just who are you?" Erik asked again. "And why do you want to help us?"

"My name is Charity. I was sent here on a mission to kill Beisch. Why he's been targeted by the American government, I don't know, and it's none of my concern."

"You are an *attentäter*, a hired killer?"

"An assassin, yes," she replied, finally comfortable with the word. "Sent by the American government. But that can never be revealed. And when everything here is done, it

will be said that you and the other farmers led a revolu-
tion against Beisch and his men."

Erik considered it a moment, then a slow grin spread
across his broad features, "One of my field hands has been
ordered to go into town and bring Beisch here after the
sun rises."

CHAPTER THIRTY-SEVEN:

Karl was awakened by one of the sentries, just before dawn. His sleep had been restless, thinking about the girl just a few hundred yards away. She'd protested, and fought like a little jaguar— but in the end he'd simply overpowered her and taken what would soon be his to enjoy, anyway.

Twice during the night, noises had awakened half the camp. Both times it had been only crocodiles catching wayward tapirs as they went to the river to drink. The whole camp had been nervous at dusk; now they just looked tired and bored.

The babo had instructed him to send one of the farmers on the ATV, an hour after the sun rose. The leader wanted to inspect the camp, along with Leon Himmel. Karl had chosen the last watch, so that he would be in the tower when the leader arrived. But just now, all he wanted was to have Jenifer again. He'd found it quite enjoyable, the way she'd struggled.

He rose and stretched, looking in the direction of Wirth's house, before walking toward the river to relieve his bladder. When he got back to the camp, he went to the nearest tower and ordered the two men to come down.

Climbing up, Karl looked out across the field on the other side of the wall. Though the sun hadn't cleared the jungle canopy yet, it was already light enough to make out details on the far side of the field. Behind him, beyond the farmer's plants, he saw no movement around the houses, and no lights on. Karl thought this unusual, as he'd always imagined farm workers to be active before daylight.

Afraid of their own shadows, Karl thought.

Below in the camp, the men began to stir, as the cook went about stoking the fire to cook eggs and meat that one of the men had raided from the farmers' pens. The meat was from several peccaries, a small indigenous pig that the farmers raised in a communal pen.

Half the men were sitting on the ground, near the fire, and Karl noted that most hadn't bothered to carry their rifles out of their tents. He was about to yell down at them, when movement to the east caught his eye.

From the first dozen or so rows of corn, several farmers stepped out into the open; at the forefront was Erik Wirth. More men came out of the rows, all of them carrying rifles. This wasn't alarming to Karl, as he knew none of them had any cartridges for their guns. The hunt was still a few days away and he hadn't distributed any ammunition. But his men didn't know this.

"Aleksander!" Wirth shouted, loud enough to be heard all over the camp.

The men below all turned toward the sound of Wirth's voice. The sun was just starting to peek over the trees on the other side of the river, and the farmers all had their backs to it, spreading out in a line.

One of Karl's men scrambled to his feet. He hadn't left his gun in the tent like the others. As the man brought his rifle up, Karl watched in disbelief as his head exploded, sending blood and tissue splattering onto the cook beside the fire.

"If another man moves," Wirth roared as he looked around the camp, "he too will die."

Karl realized that Wirth hadn't yet noticed that he was in the tower. He started to raise his own rifle, when he heard a noise to his left. When he looked, he saw the man in the other tower fall backward over the wall. Another man, standing at the bottom of the ladder, turned and raised his rifle, though the farmers were much too far away. Karl watched in horror as a pink mist replaced the man's head, and his body slumped to the ground.

Impossible, he thought. *The other tower is over two kilometers away.*

Karl suddenly realized that he hadn't heard any shots.

"Come down from there, *kinder!*" Wirth shouted. "This is between me and you! Do not get any more of your men killed."

When Karl looked back at Wirth, the man was staring straight at him. *How can this be?* He thought. *None of them have cartridges.*

"You are out of your mind, old man!" he bellowed, his anger boiling over. "Where did you get the cartridges?"

"Get down here now!" Wirth roared, stepping forward and shouldering his rifle. "Or I will kill you there. If anyone moves to interfere, they will die where they sit."

Below, not a single man moved. The only ones armed were the two that he'd just relieved. The farmers stood on the berm created by the annual floodwaters coming around the wall. They were slightly higher than the men in the camp, and the sun was directly behind them now. The farmers' shadows stretched almost to the tents, telling Karl that his men were blinded, looking toward the farmers on the berm.

Out of the corner of his eye, Karl saw movement to his left. The other sentry who had just come down from the tower stepped out of the corn, where he'd probably gone to take a leak. When the man saw his companion dead beside the ladder, he began to run toward the body. Amazingly, he only made it three steps before he spun and fell to the ground, a stream of red arcing from his chest as he spun. A second later, Karl heard the sickening thunk of the bullet hitting him, but still no report from a rifle.

Wood splinters suddenly flew out of the post next to Karl's head, several sticking into his face and neck.

"That was your last warning!" Wirth shouted as he took another step forward, his rifle pointed up at the tower, unmoving. "Leave your rifle and climb down!"

Slowly, Karl began climbing down the ladder, leaving his rifle in the tower. *I will kill this old man with my own two hands*, he thought. *The others will then scatter and I will kill the old man's wife and take Jenifer again. This time, in the old man's own bed.*

When Karl reached the ground, Wirth moved toward him, lowering his rifle, but still pointing it directly at him. "Order your men to carry their rifles by the barrel in their left hand, one at a time, and place them on the ground here."

Quickly, the farmers fanned out into a half circle around the camp, rifles trained on the men sitting around the fire. "I know you do not have any cartridges, old man. Whatever trickery you are using will not work."

Karl's eyes went to Rolph, sitting by the fire. The man's body was tensed, like a Jaguar ready to pounce. One hand was on the pistol in his belt, watching Karl intently for any signal. Karl nodded slightly and Rolph came to his feet, bringing the revolver out of his belt.

Wirth turned the barrel of his rifle and fired a single shot, the loud boom of the Winchester splitting the quiet morning air like thunder. Several birds roosting in the trees, took off in panicked flight.

Karl couldn't believe his own eyes. Rolph froze, his pistol halfway up, and looked down at the blood spreading across his shirt in the middle of his chest. He looked over at Karl, his eyes already blank, then crumbled to the ground, one leg going into the fire.

The sound of Wirth's bolt chambering another round, brought Karl back to the reality of the moment. As if in slow motion, the spent cartridge from Wirth's rifle flipped end over end and fell into the dust beside him.

"How many more men are you going to cause to die?" Wirth asked. "Tell them to bring their guns out now!"

Slowly, Karl turned and looked at his remaining men— already reduced by a fourth. "Do as he said."

One by one, men rose and went to their tents to retrieve their rifles, carrying them carefully by the barrel and depositing them in front of Wirth, then returning to the group.

When all the rifles lay on the ground at Wirth's feet, the farmer said, "Back away from the camp and stand over there by the door."

Several men turned and looked at Karl, questioningly. He nodded, and the men moved away from the camp, toward the door. "Open it," a woman's voice shouted, seeming to come from the edge of the cornfield.

Karl watched as a pile of leaves slowly rose and took on the shape of a moss covered tree stump, pointing a branch at the men. Several of his men murmured, as the tree swept a thick, moss-covered branch up and pulled the leaves from the top of the form, revealing the head and face of a beautiful dark-haired woman.

The woman started toward his men, still pointing what Karl now realized to be some kind of rifle at them. "I said, open the damned door," the woman hissed.

One of the men, whether out of bravery against a single woman, or stupidity, charged at her. Her long rifle barrel spat flame, making only a quiet pfft sound. This was followed instantly by the nearly silent mechanical sound of the rifle ejecting a very large spent cartridge and chambering another. The man charging her was yanked backward. As if attached to a mighty spring, he was lifted off his feet, landing with a dull thud in the dirt.

"I am not in the habit of repeating orders," the woman said in broken German, pointing the rifle menacingly.

The men at the door panicked, all of them trying to lift the large timber at once, then pushing the door open as the woman approached. "Out," she told them and they hurried through the door.

The strange woman approached the door and ordered them to close it, as Karl watched helplessly. When the door was pushed closed, she leaned her rifle against the wall, lifted the large timber and dropped it back into place.

"You've been voted off the island," the woman said in English, pulling apart the top of the strange looking suit, with a ripping sound. She shrugged out of it and pulled the bottom part of the garment off, revealing a shapely body dressed in a tight-fitting black sleeveless shirt, black pants, and black boots. She draped the suit over one arm and picked up her rifle, then walked toward where Karl stood.

The strange woman stopped in front of him, her eyes venomous with hate.

"Who are you?" Karl asked in English.

"Charity Styleski," the woman replied. "The Polish Jew who is now going to kill your leader. I don't know what Erik's plans are for *you*, but if it was up to me, I'd have you take off your pants and walk out far enough into the river for the piranha to snack on your little *schwanz*, you fucking pedophile."

The woman turned and walked over to stand beside Wirth. She spoke something to him, but Karl didn't hear. Wirth pointed at one of his men and made a circling motion with his finger pointed up. The man ran toward Karl's ATV, started it, and roared away, heading toward the trailhead and town.

CHAPTER
THIRTY-EIGHT:

Martin Beisch sat in a chair on the porch, sipping coffee. He didn't appear to have a care in the world, comfortable that the great wall would keep out any intruders.

In the chair next to him, Leon looked at his watch. "He should be here any time."

As if by his own order, Leon heard the sound of Aleksander's machine slowly approaching the house. It came to a stop a few meters from the steps and the man climbed out. "Aleksander said you wished to visit the farm?"

"I wish to visit the camp of my security people," the babo corrected him, rising from his chair.

Leon stood up and followed the leader down the steps. "Get in the back," Leon told the farmer, as he stepped around to the driver's side.

The man shrugged and went to the back of the machine, as Leon climbed in and started the engine. The babo climbed in the passenger seat, and Leon put the ATV in gear. He maneuvered slowly around the yard, waiting until he was on the dirt path before accelerating.

It took only twenty minutes to reach the farm. Leon passed the home of the man who ran the farm, Erik Wirth. Turning to go around the crops, he saw the farmer's wife and daughter standing on the porch. Leon had thought about claiming the girl, but Karl had beat him to it and challenging that man was out of the question.

Rounding the edge of the farm, Leon was impressed that all of Karl's men were formed in two lines, with Karl and Wirth standing several meters apart next to one of the large tents. A dark-haired woman Leon didn't recognize stood off to one side as he brought the machine to a stop between the two rows of men.

Shutting off the engine and climbing out, Leon looked around at the serious faces of Karl's security team. Glancing at Karl and Wirth, he thought it unusual that the farmer held a hunting rifle, but Karl's hands were empty.

The babo extricated himself from the vehicle, dusting off his tan slacks. He looked from Karl to the woman, and then back to his head of security. "Who is this woman?"

Leon had a bad feeling about all of this. The woman, wearing a black sleeveless shirt and black pants, strode toward Beisch. She was very attractive and Leon looked her up and down. It was then that he noticed that she had a pistol holstered on her right hip.

"Are you Martin Beisch?" the dark-haired woman asked. "The babo?"

Ignoring her, Beisch asked again, "Who is this woman, Karl? And why are none of your men in the towers?"

Leon slowly stepped away to his left. The woman stopped a meter in front of the babo. "I will ask you again," she said, her words coming out as though German wasn't her native language. Indeed, she looked more like the Indian farmers to the south, only taller. "Are you the babo, Martin Beisch?"

Slowly, the babo turned and faced the woman. "Yes, I am the babo," he sneered. "And since my security man seems to have lost his tongue, who are you and why are you here?"

"My name is Styleski," the woman said in a quiet, even tone. "My grandfather was driven out of his homeland by Nazis, simply because of his religion."

Beisch's eyes widened. "You are the *ferkel* of a *Juden-schwein*?"

The woman spun suddenly, leaping into the air. Leon watched as she moved in a blur, one leg whipping out and catching the babo on the side of the head, sending him toppling sideways.

Landing lightly and drawing her pistol, the woman shouted, "Say it again!" Before Leon could even touch his own pistol, the woman pointed hers at Beisch and thumbed the hammer back. "Call me a pig one more time."

The babo struggled slowly up to one knee, holding a hand to the side of his face and looking at this strange woman, anger spreading across his features. "Kill this whore!" he ordered Karl.

The security man didn't move as Beisch fought to get to his feet. A split lip left a trickle of blood on his chin. The fact that a Jew woman held a gun pointed at his face seemed to have no effect on the babo.

"I do not know where you came from," Beisch said. "But here, women are property. And a Jew woman would be put in the pens to be bred like the rest of the sows."

The gun in the woman's hand barely made a sound. A small flame shot from the end of the long barrel and it jerked up slightly, before coming to rest pointing at Leon's face.

The babo's head jerked backward and he fell back at Leon's feet, a bloody hole in the center of his forehead.

"With just two fingers," the woman said, "slowly take that gun from your holster and toss it on the ground."

Leon did as he was ordered, dropping his old-west style Colt .44 onto the ground. The woman bent and picked it up then looked off to her left. "Is this the man?" she asked in American English.

Leon noticed the shaman, Navarro, standing next to what he now realized were the farmers, not Aleksander's security people.

"Yes," the man replied, also in English. "He killed one of my neighbor's field workers, a small boy of eleven summers. He used that very gun. Then he had his men throw the boy's lifeless body to the caribes."

"Do the same with your boss," the black-clad woman said, pointing at the babo's body with the barrel of her pistol.

Slowly, so as not to give her any reason to shoot, Leon went to the dead leader. Grabbing him under the arms, he half-carried and half-dragged the body toward the river. At the bank, he stopped and looked at the water in horror. Several bodies floated there, the red water roiling around them in what he recognized as the frenzied feeding of the big black piranha.

Breathing heavily from the exertion, and holding back the bile rising in his throat, Leon turned to the woman standing above him. "I will need help throwing the body in."

"Perhaps in a moment," she said, motioning with her gun. "Follow me."

One of the farmers stepped forward and prodded him in the back with a hunting rifle. Leon followed the woman back up the hill as she holstered her pistol.

Karl seemed to be fuming with anger now. Leon knew he would feel bad for having failed his leader. Turning to Wirth, Karl growled, "Put down that gun and I will kill you in a fair fight with my bare hands." Then he grinned at the farmer and added, "Just as I did your three whining sons."

Wirth turned and tossed his rifle to a man standing behind him. In a flash, Karl attacked. He took a giant stride forward, closing the gap between himself and Wirth, swinging a big right hand just as the larger man turned back around. The blow landed solidly on the older man's chin.

To his credit, Wirth didn't go down, only staggered sideways from the force of the blow. When he stopped, he turned toward Karl, spitting blood. "You hit like a girl and fight like a coward."

Karl stepped forward again, feinting with a left jab and then bringing another roundhouse right toward Wirth's chin. The farmer was ready for it this time, and not fooled by the sloppy left-handed jab. He easily blocked Karl's punch with his left forearm, bringing his right fist up into the security man's belly.

Air whooshed from Karl's lungs, the powerful punch nearly lifting him off the ground. Wirth hit him again in the same place, and Karl doubled over, unable to draw a breath.

Snatching him by the hair, Wirth lifted his head and drew back his own right hand. "This is for my boys!" he roared, as he struck Karl with a fist that might as well have been a sledgehammer.

Karl went down to one knee, but Wirth wasn't through. "And this is for what you did to my daughter," he growled, bringing his bloody right fist down hard on the side of Karl's face.

The security man dropped face first into the dirt. His body twitched once and then he was still. Wirth spun and pointed a bloody finger at Leon. "Drag this carcass to the river, as well!"

Leon looked slowly around at the men and the one woman, all staring at him. With even more difficulty, he took Karl's legs up under his arms and slowly dragged him down to where the babo's lifeless body lay at the water's edge. He wasn't sure, but he thought Aleksander was still alive; his chest seemed to be moving slightly.

Wirth, the strange dark-haired woman, and the old shaman followed Leon, who stood wheezing from the exertion. "He is not dead," he said, between breaths.

Wirth bent and grabbed Karl by the belt with one hand and by the collar with his other. In an amazing display of sheer power, he lifted the smaller man up to his chest, then slowly pressed him high above his head. Wirth took one step into the water and heaved, sending Karl flying toward where the bodies of the other men were being picked clean by the ravenous fish.

The sudden splash scattered the school for a moment, before they realized it wasn't a threat and went back to their grisly task. Karl's body suddenly jerked and he began splashing around, before rising to his feet. A small piranha was latched to the side of Karl's neck, flopping its tail as its teeth dug deeper into the man's flesh.

Karl screamed in terror and agony, his hands going not to his neck, but beneath the water to his crotch, as he toppled over sideways. He thrashed around for a few more seconds and then stopped, his blood mixing with the blood of the others. His body floated face down and was jerked slightly by the terrible fish as they ripped out large chunks of flesh with their razor sharp teeth.

"Now the babo's body," the woman said, drawing her pistol again.

"I am not as strong as Wirth," Leon said. "I cannot lift him."

She pointed the pistol menacingly at his head and hissed, "Drag it into the water."

Leon looked at her, horrified, the realization of what she meant slowly sinking in. He had only one chance and that was to run. But there was no place to run to. The farmers had surrounded him in a semi-circle.

Leon did the only thing he could do. Slowly, he grabbed the body of his friend and leader of the community. Getting his hands under the arms of the lifeless body, Leon began walking backward, angling slightly toward where the wall ended a few meters from shore.

When the water reached the top of Leon's leather boots, he heaved Beisch's body to his right, where the large black piranhas were feasting on what was left of Karl. At the same time, he dove to the left, striking out as fast as he could swim for the end of the great barrier.

If I can only make it around the wall, he thought, swimming for all he was worth.

Amazingly, he made it. Flipping over onto his back, safe at least from the guns, Leon swam in a modified back stroke toward shore, keeping his hands below the water, so as not to splash and attract the deadly fish.

The last thing Leon saw, just before darkness closed around him, were the giant teeth of a waiting crocodile.

EPILOGUE

Charity checked with the hotel desk clerk, who told her that Rene had checked out late the night before, probably before she'd left to meet Napier.

After the killings by the river, she'd radioed the one-eyed giant and, true to his promise, he'd arrived within minutes. She'd offered Vicente a ride back to his own farm, which he'd shrugged off, saying that he wanted some time with the farmers to discuss the future for the area.

The men Charity had sent to the other side of the wall were nowhere around when she'd retrieved her pack from where she'd left it by the log at the edge of the jungle. Unarmed, they faced at least a day-long hike through the dangerous jungle to any kind of civilization. If they were lucky, one or two might make it. She doubted any of them would.

When she'd retrieved her pack and ghillie suit, and was finally boarding Napier's boat, the old shaman had been sitting beside the camp fire with Wirth. The two were sharing the old man's pipe.

The ride back to Trinidad had been at nearly full throttle all the way, and only took a couple of hours. Charity had sat on the small seat in front of the console, not wishing to talk to Napier about what had happened at the settlement. Once they were clear of the river, the wind had buffeted her and the salt spray had mixed with the tears on her face, both stinging her eyes.

Instead of going to the dock they'd left from, Napier had taken the boat all the way to the hotel's pier. Before they'd arrived, she'd stowed all her gear and called Devon to pick her up. He'd been waiting at the hotel entrance when she got there. She'd tossed her backpack and long fly rod case in the backseat, telling him she'd be just a moment, then she'd gone inside to inquire about Rene.

She wasn't sure how she felt about his being gone, but part of her was relieved. On the short trip to the airport, she composed an email to Stockwell and saved it, saying only that she'd accomplished the mission with help from the people of the settlement, and she was flying back to her boat in the Caymans to relax for a week or two.

During her preflight check, her phone vibrated in her pocket, alerting her of a new message. A saved message from Stockwell congratulated her on a job well done. He said to leave the helicopter with the FBO in the Caymans and they would keep it in storage.

Though she was exhausted, she planned to fly straight through and sleep in the bird for a few hours when she refueled in Saint Croix. She wanted only to get back to her boat, sail off somewhere, and find a quiet lagoon to anchor and rest up.

When she arrived at the Cayman airport the next afternoon, a taxi whisked her to the marina where *Wind Dancer* was docked. She settled up with the Dockmaster, threw off the lines and slowly left the harbor. She had no particular destination, nor even direction, in mind.

As she approached Rum Point, another sailboat half a mile ahead of her turned west, so she turned east. Toggling the switches, she unfurled the sails and, and as the wind filled them, she shut down the engine. She adjusted her course a little south of east, to avoid going anywhere near the Cuban coast, then set the autopilot.

As the sun slowly slipped toward the horizon behind her, painting the clouds a rusty red color, Charity walked along the port side, checking her equipment. She stood at the bow for several minutes, leaning against the forestay as she scanned the empty sea ahead of her.

She still had no idea where she was going, wanting only distance from where she had been. She knew that ahead of her lay the island of Jamaica and, beyond that, Hispaniola.

Montego Bay might be a good place to start, she thought. *I can lose myself among the thousands of tourists.*

THE END

If you'd like to receive my twice a month newsletter for specials, book recommendations, and updates on coming books, please sign up on my website:

WWW.WAYNESTINNETT.COM

THE CHARITY STYLES
CARIBBEAN THRILLER SERIES

Merciless Charity
Ruthless Charity
Heartless Charity (Spring, 2017)

THE JESSE MCDERMITT
CARIBBEAN ADVENTURE SERIES

Fallen Out
Fallen Palm
Fallen Hunter
Fallen Pride
Fallen Mangrove
Fallen King
Fallen Honor
Fallen Tide
Fallen Hero (Winter, 2016)
Rising Storm (Summer, 2017)

The Gaspar's Revenge Ship's Store is now open. There you can purchase all kinds of swag related to my books.
WWW.GASPARS-REVENGE.COM

AFTERWORD

I have so many people who contributed to this book, that I need to thank. As always, first and foremost come my wife and family. Without their support, I probably would never have completed the first novel, let alone this eleventh one.

My beta readers do a superb job in pointing out inconsistencies in my writing, and are a huge blessing in many technical aspects. Many thanks to Dana Vilhen, Karl Schulte, Alan Fader, Chuck Hofbauer, Ron Ramey, Debbie Kocol, Jeanne Gelbert, Katy McKnight, John Doe, and Mike Ramsey. Without your help, this book wouldn't be nearly as good. Particular gratitude is owed to my close friend, Army Warrant Officer Paul Deaver. Paul is an active duty Apache helicopter pilot, and helped enormously with the flight scenes.

I also want to thank the whole Down Island Press team for an exceptional job getting this book to print on schedule. Editor extraordinaire Tammi Labrecque, with Larks and Katydids, and proofreader Donna Rich worked many hours fixing all my many mistakes; thank you both for your dedication to the written word. I also owe a lot of thanks to Colleen Sheehan of WDR Book Design for the quality formatting job and Shayne Rutherford of Wicked Good Book Covers, for an exceptional job with the book's cover.

Many of my readers contributed ideas and suggestions for this book. Thank you Bob Morrison, Gene Dugan, Patrick Burns, Sam Wagner, Chuck Hofbauer, Len Capelli, Carl Nielson, Gray Davis, Leslie Bright, Bill Black, Patrick McBurnette, James Sinnett, LaVon Ritter, and Cliff Barth. A special thanks to Peter Asselin for suggesting Thurman Napier's very unique boat name, *Wipe This*.